Mothersland

Mothersland

By Shahzoda Samarqandi

Translated by Shelley Fairweather-Vega,
after the Russian version translated from Persian
by Yultan Sadykova (Red Intellect, 2019)

Bloomington, Indiana, 2024

Cover design used by permission of Red Intellect, adapted for the American edition by Tracey Theriault.

ISBN: 978-089357-527-4

Library of Congress Cataloging-in-Publication Data

Names: Samarqandī, Shahzādah, 1975- author. | Fairweather-Vega, Shelley, translator.
Title: Mothersland / Shahzoda Samarqandi ; translated by Shelley Fairweather-Vega, after the Russian version translated from Persian, by Yultan Sadykova (Red Intellect, 2019).
Other titles: Zamīn-i mādarān. English
Description: Bloomington, Indiana : Three String Books, 2024. | Summary: "A novel on the bond between a mother and daughter in late Soviet-era Uzbekistan"-- Provided by publisher.
Identifiers: LCCN 2024009304 | ISBN 9780893575274 (paperback)
Subjects: LCGFT: Novels.
Classification: LCC PK6562.29.A46 Z2613 2024 | DDC 891.73/5--dc23/eng/20240325
LC record available at https://lccn.loc.gov/2024009304

Slavica Publishers
Indiana University
1430 N. Willis Drive
Bloomington, IN 47404-2146
USA

[Tel.] 1-812-856-4186
[Toll-free] 1-877-SLAVICA
[Fax] 1-812-856-4187
[Email] slavica@indiana.edu
[www] http://www.slavica.com/

Mama lies at the edge of a field at noon on a summer day, face to the sky. She is giving birth to me. A beefy man paces back and forth nearby and cannot do a thing to help. That is the chairman of our collective farm. Mama clutches the thin stalk of a cotton plant tightly in both hands. She has clenched her teeth and does not make a sound. It wouldn't be good to demonstrate weakness in the presence of a man. She had asked the chairman to be nearby, somewhere not far off, but not to come any closer. It wouldn't be good. People would gossip. Most importantly, my papa would be angry if he found out some man had looked up his wife's skirt.

My sister runs up, sobbing, and lets everything she managed to carry here tumble down onto the ground next to Mama. Mama is now lying quietly, legs and arms outstretched, protecting the thing she has nestled in her skirt. She spreads a kerchief on the ground and places me on top of it.

From the other edge of the field, an old woman approaches, limping slightly, and the chairman helps her across the canal. She lifts her trembling hands to the heavens and begins praying loudly.

This is all that my sister remembers of the scene in which I made my first appearance. And the old woman, even though she arrived too late to help Mama, still considers herself my midwife. She says, "When I got there, you were on a green kerchief, belly button still tied to your mother, like you had grown straight from the ground. And you were exactly the same color as a pumpkin." My midwife nicknamed me the wild one. She always said, "The earth was your first cradle, and the sky was the ceiling over your head. You'll never be tamed."

That same old woman named me Aftab, which means "sunshine." I was glad. "Sunshine" is much better than "pumpkin," isn't it? Naturally, my father was unhappy, but the women, who presented a much more united front amongst themselves than they ever did with the men, didn't listen to him. They insisted on calling me Aftab until that finally became my name. And so it happened that I have two mothers and two fathers. The kolkhoz chairman is convinced that if he hadn't come to mother's assistance, I would never have survived, and the midwife thir the same. But Mama says I pushed myself out without anybody's help, without too much torment and pain, and took in the view of the sunset from between her legs. Mama always takes a poetic view of everything around her. Exactly the opposite of me. I'm a realist, like Papa. Maybe because I've never seen life act with any courtesy. I was born in a field like a pumpkin, then I was planted on an old kolkhoz tractor and brought home. Is that any way to begin a human life? If that's how a person begins, how can she expect to end? God help her.

But it's the truth that when I got older, they handed over the farm's only tractor to me, all because of this story. Not any of the strapping young men, but me, a skinny, awkward little girl. Their reasoning was that ever since my birth, the earth had been more fruitful, and we had been meeting the annual cotton quota on time. My arrival brought joy and good fortune to everyone—except myself.

I lift my head from the notebook. Forty years have passed since these notes were made, and in so many years, my mother had never shown them to a stranger. Until today, when the Russian man walked into our house and ignored the cup of tea I brought him. He looked at the teacup, then at me, then at my mother, and then at the cup again. When I had brought him that cup, my other arm folded across my breast in respect, the tea in it had been almost boiling. He propped his elbows on the table and looked. When he lifted the cup to his lips, the tea was no longer steaming. It was cold. But our guest's eyes flashed brighter than before.

"Do you have a family photo album?"

Mama looked at me. "He'd probably like the diary, instead, wouldn't he?" she asked. I nodded. "Go and get it."

The man went on shooting secretive looks at me and my mother in turn. He didn't look at his teacup again.

I stood up and pushed my chair in, which I never do. I don't know why this guest was making me so upset. Why push in a chair I'm only going to sit in again in a minute? Mama was agitated as well. There was someone sitting across from her, taking a lively interest in her.

In the doorway, I turned to look at Mama. I didn't understand why she wanted to reveal the diary to this stranger. She had never even shown it to Papa. I went into the library and started searching.

The notebook wasn't where I had left it last time. I came back empty-handed. Even before I walked into the room, my mother said, "On the bed."

She didn't say which bed. I went straight to her bedroom. The diary was there on the quilt. Obviously, Mama had been preparing for this. I leafed through it. All the pages were there.

Our guest looked through the whole diary, beginning to end, and handed it to me: "Read some." I shot a glance at Mama. She looked calm, even pleased. I started to read from the very first page.

"Mama lies at the edge of a field at noon on a summer day, face to the sky. She is giving birth to me...."

The man lifted one finger. I stopped reading. I translated into Russian for him, without waiting for him to say anything. He looked at Mama. He kept looking for a long time, as if he wanted to read all the wrinkles on her face.

"Is it the truth?"

Mama nodded. "Everything in there is my own life story."

The man rose to his feet and walked across the living room. He might have been weighing his options: we'll start with that scene, and then... He turned toward Mama again and asked, "And where is this field?" I stood up and gripped the back of my chair. I knew where it was! Mama went to that field two or three times every year and took a long walk around.

She looked at our guest. "Yes, Mahtab will show you the way, if you like."

No more than two people had ever read that notebook. Mama and I read it constantly. When Mama felt sad, she took it out and reread the passages about her mother. But I liked to read the chapters about *her.* Again I wondered about the Young Poet. She has never told me who the Young Poet is. Do I know him? Is he still alive? Her only answer, when I ask, is that he was a poet who was young back then.

She didn't like it when I pressed her. "So much has happened since then... It's better to let it lie in the tomb of time." The Russian man came here to open that tomb.

Mama slowly walked around the red tractor, explaining something to the driver. She always kept one hand at the small of her back. When she wanted to straighten up, she set her palm there and pressed a bit. Any time her spine felt weak, that hand went behind her back, and her fingers clenched, like the talons of a bird in flight. Mama had gotten older—older and tormented by aches and pains. But she tried not to let on. She always rode with the film crew and was more cheerful than ever. She even helped them get their filming permit and a small plot of the cotton field allocated for the shoot. She brought the tractor in from the central station. And she always rushed to defend the film, saying, "In order to preserve history, you need to re-create it."

Everyone was always running, hurrying, fussing, and everyone I saw was completely absorbed in their work. Only the director, pensive and quiet, spent any time deeply contemplating the action around him. If he had been hosting a wedding banquet, he'd be the kind who knew everything that happened, even behind the scenes. The expression on his face changed every time he glimpsed a new detail. He crossed his arms over his chest and stared hard at everyone there on location.

Most often, my eyes were trained on him. He was always spinning a pen in his hands, and he tended to fiddle with his dark mustache before he wrote anything. At first, I thought that he was sniffing his fingernails, but later, after looking more closely, I realized he was twisting the ends of his mustache where they sharpened to a point. It was his favorite habit. Soon as he felt someone looking at him or emerged from his own thoughts, he ran a hand over his face and smoothed his tousled whiskers.

I stood up and absentmindedly brushed off my skirt. A cotton field is a grim, exhausting place, a thing I had always seen day in, day out on television, reigning over the front pages of the newspapers, all year round. Sometimes you flip through the channels, and every one of them is reporting on cotton—the volumes harvested, the speed of progress, the effect of the weather on the harvesting process, and on and on.

Mama wrote that cotton, like a pet child, always demanded everyone's attention. From cultural figures to doctors, from university students to schoolchildren, from the media to the arts, everyone and everything depended on flourishing, ever-increasing cotton yields. Cotton was society itself.

Now I was here face-to-face with this spoiled child, and I felt like grabbing its cheeks with both hands and squeezing. Until it hurt. Until it suffered as much from the pain as Mama had suffered because of it.

I reached out and plucked a boll of cotton from the house where it was born. It could be stretched into a thread like silk. I reached for another small bundle—ow, ouch. A sharp needle stabbed into me under my fingernail. A caustic pain, almost an itch, spread over my entire body. It settled under my skin like snake venom. I brought my finger to my mouth and clamped my lips over the injured place. When I sucked, the pain relented, but as soon as I relaxed my lips, the burning flared again.

The director walked up. "Close your eyes and look through your mother's eyes. Look at the field as if the whole crop still needs to be harvested, or the people will not have clothing or oil or firewood." That thought never gave Mama any peace, day or night.

I looked uncomprehendingly at the director. I walked toward the others, taking tiny steps. A question had settled into me. Why cotton? It puzzled me how interested this man was in cotton farming. He saw something in cotton that I could not. He would take a cotton boll into his hand and breathe in its scent. "Mmmm... The aroma of snow and rain!" That was something I'd never done. Or he would scoop up a handful of earth, bring it to his mouth, and taste it. He would chew on the soil and mutter to himself.

One time, he said, "The earth here smells like the sea." The sea? Before the whole story with the filming began, when I looked at a cotton field, I saw three things: the sky, the land, and the horizon. Before all that, I never bothered noticing anything that lay between them. This man found a thousand vital elements there which I could not quite grasp. I saw nothing, heard nothing, smelled nothing.

But when he spoke—in a friendly way, or sometimes angrily—I started to believe that it might be possible to have a job you perform with passion and inspiration. That must have been the first time I ever saw people spending all their days and nights in that field doing something other than picking cotton.

Whenever I used to pass people working in the field, I remember thinking they were bowing to the earth day in and day out. But this group bowed to the camera. Every second, they were busy setting it up and making adjustments. They carried it back and forth, sometimes on their shoulders, sometimes on a truck. The camera and the cotton, like a pair of idols, made people their abject subjects.

I held my hands behind my back and walked, pretending to be Mama. Mama watched me from a distance, like a burning lantern visible from everywhere. I walked closer to her. She smiled. "Dear heart, those are my old woman habits. When I was young, I walked with my back straight, head held high." Mimicking Mama wasn't difficult, but I couldn't quite get it.

Railroad tracks divided the wide field in half. The blossoming cotton covered the earth like snow. An irrigation canal ran parallel to the tracks, full of reddish water. A few members of the crew were rinsing their dirty shoes there. I could see ten or twelve camping tents perched on the earth like ladybugs, not far from two old trailers.

One of them had been assigned to me and Mama. Work came to a halt at the most brutally hot time of day, and everyone stretched out in the shade of the young cypress trees that grew along the canal. You could hear the sounds of a guitar and singing, and people clapping happily and whistling.

I went into our trailer and picked Mama's diary up from her metal cot. It got heavier every time, and every time it was more difficult to choose what part to read. Sometimes, I only leafed through it, looking at the shapes of the sentences. The words were embroidered with love across each page. I was enchanted by the attention given to each of those words, and I forgot about time. No matter what project Mama took up, she always did it with sensitivity and intelligence, in her own special style.

Closing my eyes, I inserted a finger between the pages at random. "Memories of my younger years." Years full of burning creative excitement, and of rebellion by a girl who was always in a hurry to break all the rules and violate all the traditions. A girl who felt at home with a shovel or axe in her hands, but found it outside her power to pick up a needle and sew a dress. A girl I was supposed to be fitting myself into in order to tame this wild earth.

But why wasn't I like her? Why was the kind of work my mother did easily so unbearable for me, almost impossible? I was willing, but my hands didn't seem to be listening to my brain... My hands weren't in line with my ideas, and I couldn't bring those ideas to life.

In the seven months we were apart, Mama kept my bedroom exactly how I had left it. The way I remembered it when I last closed the door behind me to head for the field where the film crew was getting swallowed up by its work. The field that swallowed up my life.

When I start looking for someone to blame, I always remember the director. The director was the one who picked me for the role of Mama as a young woman. The director was the one who managed to bring Mama's identity to life inside me during our two months of shooting. He loved that role more than all the rest, as if it were the most important discovery of his life.

I learned my lines quickly. Mama used to tell me about her younger days all the time, the days of her womanly heroism. Those stories held my own life in derision, and simultaneously they wormed their way deep inside me, weaving my roots. But it was striking how this stranger, this man, could penetrate so far into the story of my mother. She was a woman who had spent her whole life courageously battling the land.

Reading the script, I came to believe even more in my mother's heroism, and every day I discovered more ways she and I were as one. So much so that my role as her came to life inside me and flowed through my veins. The role of the first woman to put on men's trousers and turn the ignition key in the tractor.

When they printed the posters, I saw in them my mother's old photograph: a big key in her hand, one foot on the step up to the tractor, her face tan and shining, in a pose that made her look something like a majestic horse, sheer magnificence and splendor. I don't know if it was an old picture of Mama or a shot from the film set. That film had become reality for me.

Mama lay on the bed, legs crossed, paging through her diary, giving the impression that a dove had landed on her hands and was flapping its wings again and again. I knew the color and scent of that diary well. When the nights were long, I took it into my hands and searched between its wings until morning.

When Mama finished writing her story, she hid the diary among her books and said, "That's much better... As if I've let everything out." Mama was right. Once she had written out her memories, she seemed to get her second breath, and now she could breathe freely, without strain or spasm, and even her gait seemed to become lighter and smoother.

Mama was like a plane tree in whose shade men and women found shelter. There, calm and peacefulness reigned, and round-bellied half-naked toddlers played, with no worries beyond mealtime and playtime. I was there among them, bare and quiet, a head taller than everyone else. That was thanks to my long ostrich neck, which stretched out insistently whether I was running or sitting still. My mother's shadow made the earth under my feet cool when it was hot, and warm when it was cold. She was solidly built, with broad shoulders and a prominent bosom. Everything that my mother had, had come up short in me. Like a little tree growing pale and thin in the shadow of a great elm.

I wished I had Mama's calm thinking, her ability to sit down at her desk and write even among chaos. I mastered her writing style and approach, but not the spirit of her words. When Mama wrote, the words yawned and stretched; they rose up and joined together wondrously. They got up and walked. I followed them. They were tethered to my gaze like a balloon and traveled on until the point where they finally disappeared.

On some pages, Mama had glued in photographs or newspaper clippings. Pictures that reminded her of her own history.

Here is the one I like the best: a photo of a girl running across an endless field. Mama had glued that photo on the left side, and on the right, she wrote something I still remember by heart, like pleasantly babbling lines of verse.

A girl runs along the narrow canal as fast as her legs can carry her. Yes, she looks like the one you can see. But you can't see what she's carrying: a pair of scissors, a bottle of rubbing alcohol, and two clean kerchiefs under her arms.

My eyes still fixed on the photograph, I try to make out the girl's hands, to see what she's holding. Nothing. I go back to reading.

Mama writes that this is her older sister running to help her.

> *Always, when I think about this scene, I am overcome by fear. God keep her from falling on those scissors! Or I imagine the blades jostling as she runs and stabbing into her eyes, her stomach... I want to stop her: "Easy, easy, don't run so fast! Don't cry! Be careful!" But at that time, I was making my own efforts—to come into the world, where my mother and sister were waiting for me.*

Between the diary's pages, I find a piece of paper with my own handwriting. I recognize it. I remember there were many times I wrote something and hid it here. I no longer know with what sort of feeling those disjointed notes were written; they do not relate to each other in any way.

You can walk fast, you can run fast, you can get on a bike or a train or an airplane, but I prefer to sit down in the shade of a tree and fly. Into the past. And there, I'll search out the roots of the future.

Two springtimes have come and gone since this record was made. But for me, it's still warm; I still recognize this scrap of paper on the desk with its edges gone brittle, yellowed and dusty enough to remind me of the skin of some animal, flayed from its flesh and bones.

I put the notebook away between Mama's thick Soviet books and walk out. Mama is working in the kitchen. There is no sound from her cooking. If things are quiet in the kitchen, that means she is deep in thought. I cough once so as not to startle her. Without looking at me, Mama says, "You're up early today. Did you sleep well?" I hug her around the waist. "I need to go."

Yesterday, when Mama put on her nightgown and got into bed, I sat down next to her, took her hands, and kissed them.

She asked me, "Do you want to go?"

"Yes," I said. "I need to find Natasha."

Mama did not answer.

I left her, went to my room, and stretched out on my belly in bed. I put Turgenev's *First Love* on my pillow. I left the window open so if Mama needed something, she wouldn't have to get up and come find me. But I could hear the floorboards creaking and my mother's measured steps. Now Mama stood in the doorway, holding a pile of paper, and her whistling breath sounded louder than usual. When she said, "This is for you from Natasha," I jumped up. I don't know if I put the book down, or if it fell, or if I went on holding it in my hands. From Natasha! At lightning speed I untied the bundle of papers, like a wolf tearing into a bird.

Natasha had written:

> *My dear, I don't know which of the names you used during your sickness I should call you now. I don't know which name you've chosen. But it doesn't matter what you call yourself—you'll always remain in my heart as a sweet friend in love. Here are your notes. I want you to have them. I am praying for you always. Natasha. Moscow.*

Now I was more impatient than ever to see that young Russian woman. She had been by my side throughout my illness, and I hadn't seen her since the day she put my hand in Mama's and said goodbye. No telephone number, no address. All I did was wave, and she flashed her bright white smile and waved back. She waved, and the train lurched into motion like an old camel. Two more lurches, and Natasha stepped out of frame, away from the window, and disappeared.

After struggling over it for weeks, Mama knocked on my bedroom door early in the morning and came in. She sat down next to the bed and put her hand to my forehead. "Mahtab, dear heart. If you truly think you need to go, then go. Don't worry about me. I have my friends here. I'm not alone. But promise me you'll take care of yourself and come home soon."

She did not answer when I asked, "Who was that Natasha, anyway? And what about the movie? Why aren't they showing it?" She didn't seem to want to know.

What had happened with the movie? After all that inspired work by the crew, all the advertising across the country and even abroad... Mama had counseled me and encouraged me through every moment of that film. She told me to persist when I grew tired, and when all the shame and torment that came to me with my role began to hurt.

"Dear heart, listen for just a second, just hold on, sit down here, have some sherbet, listen to me. Try to imagine you're getting into that tractor for the first time, that this is the first time you've even seen a tractor. Understand? The very first time! The tractor is terrifying, it's a monster—of course you'd be scared! This is a demon standing there in front of you! And everyone around you is frightened of its voice and of the tracks it leaves. You're frightened, too! But you want to conquer your fear. Do you understand?"

For the tenth time, the makeup guy splashes water onto my face, smooths my hair and plasters it to my cheeks and forehead. I understand. "Okay, once again, let's go! Five, four, three, two... Camera!"

Fearfully I approach the tractor. Slowly I lift one foot toward the metal step. Ivan reaches out his hand. I pretend not to notice, and I try again to scramble up. It doesn't work. It's a big step. On the third time, my foot reaches, and now I'm hanging off the tractor by both hands and a foot. My other foot is still on the ground, and I'm scared, I'm truly scared to separate myself from the earth. I finally manage to haul my body into the seat. I put my hands on the steering wheel. For the fifth time in this very same shot, the director shouts. "No, no, no!"

☙ ❧

By the time Mama and I returned from the field, I could finally distinguish precisely between what was me and what was her. This was after a long quarrel with a person in a military uniform.

I was mourning unbelievably at the thought of my friends and loved ones, all of them, head to toe, and I wanted to see them all. Mama told me I hadn't spoken with them for a long time. When they came to see me, I acted distant and wouldn't respond to them.

In the sun, Mama's face turned red, and thin strands of hair stuck to it around the edges. Mama lifted her arms and fanned her armpits. She kept her mouth half open to breathe, and from time to time, she let her upper lip jut out, then her lower lip, and blew streams of air into her face. Her earrings from Bukhara seemed frightened from the breeze coming off the magazine she used as a fan, and they darted away from it in different directions. They were big earrings, seven or eight red stones in each one, framed with small coral beads. Mama always wore those earrings when she was getting dressed up in her official uniform and pinning all her medals and ribbons to her chest. The uniform was a dark shirt down to her waist and a skirt to match, coming maybe six inches below the knee. Mama had saved that uniform since Soviet times. Her hairstyle, too. She kept it swept back and twisted around her head. She always dyed her hair dark. Mama was one of those women who naturally went stout—"tetrahedral," as she liked to call it.

Mama was overjoyed that my memory had come back. She fanned herself even faster with the magazine, and said, "I hope he won't keep pestering us. I don't have any more patience for sorting things out with the police." Mama looked at me and kept talking as if with an affectionate friend. "I remembered to write down his name. We'll have to bring him some kind of gift, anyway."

Though she was trying to act cheerful, and even winked at me, I could see she was worried. She was worried that this military man who had stopped us at the edge of the field might start tailing us.

But Mama's eyes were flashing. This was the most vibrant I had seen her all year. Her eyes were transparent and playful, like seawater in the early spring.

I took a walk around outside. I looked into every nook and cranny of the yard and the house, as if I had returned after a long trip very far away. The door and front gate seemed to have settled into the earth, tucking their heads down into their shoulders against the heat and the cold. Mama's house looked like an old woman in faded clothing. Its little windows stared meekly, bashfully, at the cotton field.

I carefully slipped off my shoes and walked barefoot around the asphalt, which was ragged in places. There had been a time when I used to run from this house, barefoot like this, and Mama used to sit in the doorway and keep an eye on me... Now when she looks, I can read her thoughts: "What finally brought Mahtab's memory back? The promises I made, the alms I gave, the rags I tied to the holy tree, or my constant prayers?"

But probably what had done the trick was the fear that officer had sowed inside Mama and me. When he was taking his leave, he had suddenly embraced me and kissed my forehead. The women and children who were picking cotton at the time surrounded us and stared at me: here I was, the girl everyone hugs and kisses, the girl rubbing dirt into her eyes. She rubs it into her eyes and gives thanks, and weeps, and kisses the hand of her elderly mother.

One woman stepped forward from the crowd, squatted down, put a copper bowl between her knees, and began to crow: "If a young shoot doesn't drop on the earth, does that shoot ever sprout? That's the greatness of a human being! We sprout from humility!"

But humility hadn't lent me any greatness. On the contrary. It brought me down to the earth, then buried me inside it. Right here in this earth I was walking over now, brushing my hands over the sharp, naked stalks of the cotton plants. This was the endless field near the big canal where we had shot the movie.

When they arrived in our village, the film crew set up their tents near the canal with the red water. They brought two old trailers from the kolkhoz, one of which they gave to me and Mama, and the other to the director and three guys from the crew. That was the first time I had ever seen a movie camera up close. It was set up right there, on long rails, and followed the actors anywhere they went, keeping pace. And that was the first time I had ever seen the cotton field emerge from what seemed to be its eternal state of monotony, its alienation from the world. Now I wanted to spend all my days and nights in the field, survey all its farthest reaches. Mama says that I'm a member of a white-handed generation, people who have lost their connection to the earth. A generation that grew up pampered, like plants raised in greenhouses.

I saw the director sitting next to the canal. He was watching the current as if through Mama's eyes. He wore faded blue jeans and a t-shirt with short sleeves he had rolled up even more. The sunglasses hanging off his belt flashed. It looked as if he wanted to shut his eyes but couldn't quite make his eyelids close. A fine little wrinkle ran from the corner of each eye to his temples and concealed itself in his dark copper-colored hair.

When he noticed me standing behind him, the director stood up and brushed off the seat of his pants. He had been sitting right on the ground. He reached out that hand—the one he had used to clean his pants—to me. He gave my hand a strong squeeze and quickly let go. "Sit with me," he said, and sat down again. There was a crunching sound. He took the sunglasses off his belt and looked them over from every angle. Not broken. He hooked them over his breast pocket, lenses out.

I sat down next to him. Without looking at me, the director asked, "Where does this water flow to?" I shrugged. "Where does it begin?" I shook my head. And in fact, I didn't know, or maybe I had just never thought about it. I had never thought that even water begins somewhere and ends somewhere. His question planted itself like a seed in my mind, and it grew and blossomed. Its flowers kept bringing me new questions.

His dark mustache and hair, streaked with strands of white, slightly concealed the Russian in him. He looked more Georgian or Armenian. But his gaze sparkled like something from another world. He said I would do well to take a good walk here, between the rows of cotton plants, and try to see everything through my mother's eyes.

And so I walked, and tried to see everything that he could see. What exactly did he find so attractive about this field? Why cotton? Why Mama?

One Saturday night, we danced around the campfire. Men, women, girls, boys—everyone danced, hand in hand. I tossed off my shoes. Barefoot, I could feel the earth better. Mama sat tucked away in a corner, the fire bouncing red flashes off her face. She watched me—me and Mikhail, who were dancing together, hand in hand.

It's hard to dance in time to the music when somebody has a strong hold on your hand and pulls you left, then right, and you're trying to look him in the eye, but his eyes are invisible. Our hands touch, and we move close; one step and we're apart. That was our whole dance. Every time we came close, he said something, and then there was another step back. Closer again and his chest touched mine.

He said, "Know what?"

And I said, "No..."

We stepped back, we again came closer.

He said, "You're so innocent."

We stepped back, we again came closer.

"Beg your pardon?"

"You and your mother, too."

I stopped. "I beg your pardon!" I tried to free my hands, but he wouldn't let go.

We came closer.

"Innocence isn't always about your body. Didn't you ask me to talk to you like an adult?"

I tried again to free my hands. He wouldn't let go. He held on tighter. He laughed loudly. "Innocence means *all* of this. You know what I mean?"

I felt even more offended at how openly he was laughing.

He said that innocence had to do with more than the body—every part of your body could remain innocent or be corrupted. Your eyes and ears, hands and feet, every part. I shot him a furious glance. Insult and understanding collided and struck a spark in my eyes.

☙ ❧

When I arrived in Moscow, I went straight to the address I'd been given without stopping to think things over.

The house looked empty, and the piles of autumn leaves swept against the door made it clear that nobody had set foot here for a long time. The mail was scattered there, too, and a cat's plaintive wailing raised a sorrow inside me. Sorrow for all the joy I had felt during that whole twelve-hour ride from Samarqand to Moscow. For those twelve hours, all I could do was listen to the thumping of the wheels and look aimlessly out the window. The speed of the train made invisible threads pop into existence before my eyes as I looked, pulling closer whatever it was they saw.

I found the hospital using the address Mama had written down. It was outside of town, in a wooded area, sleeping in the snow. I walked along a path made by cars and pedestrians and couldn't tell what I was feeling. I was lost in the expanses of the gargantuan city, and Natasha seemed to be a needle in a haystack here, among all these bewildered people, ducking their heads down into their collars and walking, running, the steam puffing from their mouths into the air when they exhaled.

Like the whole city was smoking. The closer I came to the hospital, the greater the disarray in my thoughts. I didn't know if I was the hunter or the prey. I didn't know if I was drunk or tired.

I knocked on the office door and felt as if I were throwing myself into the sea, ignorant of how deep it was. A moment later, I found myself in the warm embrace of a squat, heavyset woman whose soft hands wrapped themselves familiarly behind my neck like a life jacket. "I knew you'd come!" she said as she embraced me.

I told her I was looking for a hotel and hadn't found anything yet. The woman smiled. "I knew you'd come one day, and I kept your room for you." She took a key off a hook behind the door and ushered me toward the hallway. I didn't know if I should bring my suitcase or leave it there in her office. She read my gaze and nodded. "Take it with you."

We walked down a vaguely familiar corridor. Now we were passing patient rooms. At a door numbered 112, my guide stopped. "Do you recognize it?"

I hid my eyes as well as I could. I could guess, but I couldn't remember. Something was telling me to hide the truth, to hide that I remembered little about this hospital and the time I spent here. I answered her slowly. "Yes, Room 112..."

"Oh yes, the famous Room 112!" said the woman, and when she said "famous," lights sparked in the blue of her eyes, then were quickly extinguished.

She inserted the key into the lock and turned it. Nobody had cleaned the room for a long time. The dry smell of dust was everywhere. I looked around. I couldn't believe it. This was the same room I had dreamed of so many times, back in Samarqand, and Mama had told me, "There is a room in Moscow where all the walls are full of your little-girl sketches of suns."

The padded fake leather lining the walls was covered with funny little suns. Some had eyebrows, others had big round cheeks. No two were identical. Their only similarity was that they were all the sun.

There was one wearing earrings, with triangular eyes. That sun had something devilish in its gaze. Nina Ivanovna walked over to it and touched it with one finger. "This one is my favorite."

I felt every moment I had spent drawing in this tiny room stir to life, seething inside me. The joy in my heart grew and pressed outward onto my skin and face, as if it were too big to fit inside my body.

"You left everything the way it was?"

"Yes," Nina Ivanovna answered, tears in her eyes.

"Why?" I don't know how it happened, but that "why" shot off my tongue, colorless, spiritless. Nina-hanum put her hands on my shoulders, and the shame dripped from my eyes. Shame for that "why," the answer to which I wouldn't be able to find on my own. I was worried. There was something I hadn't remembered yet.

She smiled. "You owe us three months. You left three months earlier than planned. But I knew you'd come back again, either way."

"Either way?"

"Yes. Either as a guest or as a patient. Whatever you might need from this room, you can stay here. You'll never be a stranger here..." She paused for a moment, then went on. "Not as long as I'm alive."

Nina Ivanovna had been running the hospital for many years. Ever since Mama had first come to visit me here and Nina gave her a room to stay in, they had been friends. Mama eagerly awaited her letters. Sometimes I noticed that she didn't seem in a hurry to read them—it was enough for her to see the familiar handwriting on the envelope; that calmed her. Mama could then breathe more easily. Perhaps she was thinking that, thank God, her friend was alive and well. Nina-hanum lived alone. She had lost her husband, and she had no children. But in her, just like in Mama, there was a kind of firmness and resilience, as if she were capable of turning someone's life upside down at a moment's notice, realizing, and making you realize, too, exactly who you were and what was going on in your head.

Nina-hanum had been right. I would have come back in either case. If my memory hadn't returned, Mama would have brought me here and delivered me to the Moscow doctors. But this time, I had returned with a multitude of whys, which, like a small child, I was supposed to use to learn about life.

And so Nina Ivanovna settled me into the same hospital room I had inhabited during my illness. Sometimes we ate dinner together, but those dinners were always outweighed by the amount of alcohol we consumed and cigarettes we smoked after her working day was over. She would sit there and tell me about everything. She easily untangled all the key questions; she knew how to separate one from the next, and each time, we concentrated on just one aspect of the past. But some parts of that past still remained in the shadows for me. Nina-hanum always answered my questions. Everything I wanted to know was laid out before me.

But she couldn't help me in my search for Natasha. She said, "She moved away somewhere, and I don't know anything about her." But she promised she'd try to get a message to Natasha, through colleagues and anyone else who might know her, that I was looking for her. What more could I ask from a simple human being in this world? Finding the refuge of a warm embrace in the Moscow cold felt like a miracle.

I set myself up in the room which had seemed so big and terrifying during my illness. Now, its close confines started to depress me. This was the room which had once chilled my soul, but then Natasha would come to me like the sun rising, and when she left, the darkness lowered its skirts to cover me.

I was angry at my own selfishness, angry that I had left my elderly mother alone to come search for Natasha through the streets and alleyways the locals pointed out to me, or wherever I sensed a phantom hope that she might be there.

When we had said goodbye, Mama had said she had never been in love, and since I had experienced that feeling, I ought to go and find it. Mama had a striking talent for bringing the truth into focus. She wasn't afraid of the truth. For her, love was a matter of pride. Back then, Mama had been the first one to sit down next to me and say, "I think you're in love." I was imprisoned then by my anger at Mikhail and my hurt feelings at his rude behavior, and I couldn't account for the fact that all my thoughts were about him. I soared on his kindnesses, I raged at his nastiness, and I could not get myself in hand. Never would I have called these daily squabbles love. But, very likely, he was the enemy without whom the struggle that had become my life would have had no meaning.

Mama grabbed hold of the next weed, a little vine winding its way around a cotton plant stalk, and she pulled it out at the root and gradually stood up straight. When Mama unbent, something seemed to snap in her back, and she winced from the pain, but only for a moment. She put a hand on my shoulder. "Look. This little vine is in love. It will always keep trying to wrap around the cotton plant and become one with it. They'll grow nicely together, they'll ripen, but they won't flower and will never produce fruit." Mama points toward the creek. "But look how much they flower and fruit when they keep apart from one another! Maybe they're doing it to attract each other's attention, strutting about, who knows. But when they're together, side by side, they're lazy. They suck the sap out of one another until winter comes and they both go dry."

Mama kept talking about the two plants, and I wondered if Mikhail could hear her. He was sitting a few paces away from us, talking to the cameraman. Did he understand that Mama was using those plants to talk about him and me? Did he see that today I was wearing white, and the breeze kept peeking into my collar and slipping under my skirt? Did he notice that we were both wearing white today? His shirt billowed in the wind and flapped against his back. He shone like a lantern in a dark night.

The sun was getting ready to fade out. The field was struggling to breathe. All the dark colors had died away; the light was exulting in its victory. In the hospital room, it had been the opposite: the light was crushed by the reigning darkness.

The walls were laced by inscriptions, all mixed together and turned upside down, and so was every surface of the bed. Little suns had been drawn, clumsy and childlike, over every surface of the table and chairs. The suns watched over the rue-fulness of the door and walls. Four padded walls, like four arms covered in tattoos.

I think about Natasha, about the times she sat next to me when I was ill and read to me from Mama's diary. She settled down next to the bed, and my gaze slid over her shoulders, ears, and breasts; I plunged my gaze into the blue of her eyes and tossed it up into her golden curls; I let it hang off her earrings and sent it back to her hair again. I could see the light from the window through those curls.

I lay in bed, my thoughts keeping me mired in those days, the days of my illness. In Samarqand, I had thought I remembered it all, but now, when I pace this room and the narrow hospital hallway, I feel as if I am seeing this place for the first time, opening this door and looking into the mirror across the hall for the first time.

All night long, I weighed my options of how, exactly, to ask. How could I ask them to let me into the archives? I needed the collection of recordings from the hospital video camera that hung over the door in my room, just as it had before, watching me ceaselessly.

When I think about my days of illness, my gaze always wanders to the camera. It follows me into every corner. I run a hand over the wall. Soft leather, tacked to the wall with a white nail every few inches. The leather was crowded with childlike drawings, writing and little suns. A circle with lines radiating out from it—one, two, three, four. This is the way the neighbor kids and I used to draw in the dirt with our fingers, and then we'd stomp on it to even out the earth, and then another circle and a line, line, line, line...

Several puffier places on the wall had holes in them. I stuck my finger in one. There was a soft stuffing. I dug a piece out with the tip of my finger. Cotton. Yellow cotton with that familiar scent: dust and earth. I remember my grandmother's daybed. Her trembling old hands cleaned the cotton and stuffed it into the mattress to make it soft. When you drifted off on Bibi's couch, you could smell the steppe. The smell of hardship. That's how your motherland smells, she used to say.

A stout woman walks in. Without looking, she switches on the lamp to the left of the door, and light fills the room. When I was sick, she was one of the people who used to come into the room with a smile and used to walk out with her hands covering her cheeks, wet with tears. Now I understand better why I responded to their kindness with anger and doubt. That understanding seems to coat me with a rash of shame nobody else can see, and my gaze darts this way and that.

The woman comes closer, arms open to embrace me. I stand up, trying to reassemble her forgotten face in my mind, and hug her back, lukewarm. For God's sake, what was her name?

"I'm happy to see you."

I spend a moment in her strong embrace. I am still there, in a posture made awkward by her protruding belly, when she says, "I've been thinking about you so much. I knew you'd come back one day. I knew it! The girl in love!"

She has me pinned between her heavy breasts, and twice she pulls her shoulders back, lifting my feet off the ground. Under my hands, I can feel the furrows made by her bra straps. When the hug releases me, I sway a little, but quickly regain my balance and remain on my feet. I love the way my visitor acts with such abandon, and I reproach myself for not remembering her name.

She looks me over, head to toe, and again presses me to herself, this time with only one arm. Her embrace no longer reeks of pity. "I'm glad you've gotten yourself in hand."

Since my recovery, I've been better able to tell things apart. I can see better that Russian kindness has a different color, smell, and taste. This kindness goes beyond simple customs and community understandings, and it envelops you immediately. I couldn't remember my guest's name, and for a second, I was even afraid that I had lost my memory again, God forbid. I went straight to the point. "Thank you for taking the time to come and see me, and in this cold! If you could possibly help me..."

The woman saw the worry in my eyes and knew I was trying to bring up something important. She stood up straighter. "I was the nurse for this ward. Maybe you remember, or... Do you? When you were a patient here, I came to see you two or three times every week."

Despite the fact that I still could not find her name in my memory, I felt braver, and I thanked her again and crossed my arms across my chest, gripping my own arms, as if trying to grab and strangle the shame that was creeping across my skin and pouring cold sweat down my face. My fingertips dug into my skin. If only I could expel that seam of shame inside me, brush it away like a spider. I put some hope into my voice and asked her a question. "Maybe you could help me. I came to find Natasha. I want to see her."

The woman gently unclenched my hand from my arm and locked it between her own palms. She stroked my hand. The meaning of her gestures was obscure to me. She looked me in the eye and spoke with a reassuring calmness. "That's why I've come. I will certainly help you, in every way I can." She took a photograph out of her purse, and her smile betrayed a slight feeling of pride when she put the photo in my hand. She kissed my forehead. A tear dropped from her eyelashes and rolled down the wrinkles on her face. I didn't notice my own gaze becoming fastened on that tear, following its descent. The nurse nodded at the photograph.

A thin girl with blue eyes, dressed in blue, gnawing on a black pen, frozen like a frightened fox in front of the camera's lens. Everything in the picture is covered with writing: the walls, the girl's skirt, the bed, her knees, her arms. Writing crowded in, no edge or end to it, like tattoos. There is so much of it that if you didn't know that girl, you'd never know if all that writing had been done in real life, before the picture was taken, or after, on the photograph itself.

☙ ❧

Hi.

I forgot your name again. I'm sorry. I'm worried that you didn't come today. I hope you'll come tomorrow. I'm sorry, yesterday I didn't feel well, I could barely lift my head. What did you say then? I can't remember. Maybe you said you weren't coming today. Maybe you're not coming at all anymore... I pray that when I open my eyes tomorrow, you will be sitting next to me.

A crumpled piece of paper. Probably I put it under my pillow or my mattress. Like all the other pages I wrote during my illness.

I stand up and walk across the hospital basement, across the storage room. The reels are still turning. This must be the third tape I've watched. But all the scenes look alike. I think about the day I said goodbye to Natasha, and Mama squeezed my hand tight. She said, "We'll be in that woman's debt until we're in the grave."

I look at the video recording. Natasha is sitting next to my bed again, observing me. I hold a pen and never take my eyes off the paper. She says, "I'm Natasha. What's your name?" The girl answers, "Oh, right... Natasha! Why am I always forgetting? I don't know." She can never wait until I remember her name myself. "You write well. Keep writing."

The girl thanks Natasha for the paper and pen she brought. Without looking her visitor in the eyes, she says, "I'm afraid. I've been afraid for a long time now." For a while, she says nothing. "What are you afraid of?" Natasha takes the girl's hand. "What if one day I wake up and realize I've forgotten how to write, too?" She tugs on her childlike ears. "I couldn't sleep last night. I wrote the names of all the people I can remember." She pulls her notes out from under her pillow and hands them to Natasha. "Can you take these with you? They'll get stolen here." Natasha takes the pile of pages from the girl and straightens it. "I'll keep them safe. When you get better, you can take them back. Don't worry. Can I read them?" The girl nods. Natasha reads aloud from the top page in her hands.

"I've been here a long time now. In this four-meter room with a window overlooking the garden, and a door leading out that I never want to walk through. I'm afraid of the narrow hallway. I'm afraid when the fat cleaning woman walks by. She doesn't see me. As if I don't exist." Natasha stops reading and puts a hand on the girl's shoulder.

I tear my eyes away from the recording and try to remember those days. The days when I truly was afraid, when the only thing I hadn't forgotten was the feeling of fear. But fear of what?

I lean against the wall and gradually, slowly, straighten my bent back. My eyes follow the fat woman. If only she would hurry up and step into one of those doorways and disappear! Then I'll run as fast as I can and... I think: but why did I ever leave my room? Where did I want to go?

Everyone I've run into in the hall seems to know me, but why don't I recognize anyone? It's as if the people here swap out their faces and bodies every day, or else they look so much alike that, even now, I can't remember their names.

Every time she walks into the room, Natasha introduces herself. Even if she's already done it a thousand times. I ask, "Don't you get tired of that?" And with her permanent, innocent smile, she answers, "Not at all. I mean, I don't know whether or not you'll remember. It's better to stick to a routine." She raises her eyebrows, as usual, and you can't figure out what her face is expressing. You don't know if she's laughing at you just then, if you're annoying her, or if she's trying hard to conceal her own sadness. And she pastes a smile on top of all that, so you believe what she says. A strange girl.

Yesterday, another woman came to see me. She spoke cheerfully as she handed me a plastic bag. "I knew you'd come one day, and I kept this for you." Expecting nothing, guessing nothing, I opened the bag.

Two white sheets completely covered in writing. It was extremely difficult to make out the words. I spread the sheets out on my bed and stared at them until I believed this truly was my handwriting, and I had once written all of this, in a state strange and alien to me. This writing was about a life that was not mine.

That same morning, Nina Ivanovna knocked on my door. I was lying in bed. I don't know for how many hours I had overslept. I was still dressed in the clothing I had been wearing a week ago, when I walked into the hospital. Jeans and a polo shirt, which seemed to fit tighter with every passing day. My fear of the cold was always with me. I was scared of catching a chill and getting stuck again in this bed, in this oppressive hospital room. It still lurked in my memory, this hospital, and it was full of horrors. Nightmares that had grown out of Mama's diary and tattooed themselves on the doors and walls of this room—the tiny room I couldn't leave, even if I wanted to.

Papers were piled on the table and the floor. Next to the chair was the little suitcase I had opened the day I arrived, clothing and toiletries mixed up in a heap inside it. I had hung two or three pairs of pants and a jacket over the back of the chair. Two light-blue scarves were draped over the headboard. A three-sided flowerpot sat on the windowsill, ready for a flower. I had slid two pairs of shoes under the bed.

I felt ungraceful and ineffective. It was pointless to search for a woman who would have sent me some news if she wanted to, or left her address with any of these nice people. I was getting the feeling that Natasha never wanted to see me again. Otherwise, why hadn't she written anything about herself in that letter? All the secrecy of her life planted despair inside me. It was making me want to wash my hands of the past, go home, and let my future, too, crumble to dust—alongside my elderly mother—tortured by questions.

I lay in the bed with all these confused, discouraging thoughts. A heavy listlessness filled my body, pinning me even more securely to the bed. This always happens on days when nothing in the world offers any kind of value and it's pure joy to huddle in a ball under the covers.

I didn't want to open the door at all. I walked to the door hoping that Nina-hanum would tell me what she wanted without coming in and then go. I waited a bit. She called my name again and pronounced it in a way that said, "I know you're in there. Open up." Warily, I opened the door a crack, the width of a narrow book's spine, so that her gaze couldn't wriggle its way in. As if there were a naked man in my room. She held a letter in her hand. "Can you stop by my office? I need to talk to you."

Her windows faced the sunset, and the room was filled with a soft light. A clump of white carnations sat prettily in a dark red vase on the desk. Nina-hanum was in her office chair. She stood up and walked around the desk. She picked up the letter—the same one she had been holding an hour ago. "This is your official permission to use the archives."

My cheeks flushed red. Now I could look at pictures from the days of my illness, and the knots would come untangled, one by one, in my tired, dusty mind.

As of today, every existing photograph of me or Natasha, everything we had written, would be at my disposal. So would the recordings I've been wandering through, dreamlike, all week, picking apart the tiny threads of memory. My memories had returned, but they were in terrible disorder due to how weak my mind had been, a disorder that was parched and anguished.

On the other hand, I hadn't known all that much to begin with that I could forget. Not about Natasha, anyway. I realized that was true when we returned from the doctors' meeting and Nina-hanum said, "Don't be shy. Ask anything you want." I wanted to ask about Mikhail. But I said, "Tell me about Natasha. Tell me everything you know about her."

She took my hand. She looked me in the eye. "Natasha was a good person. I don't know what happened to make her up and leave like that... But she was good. Don't ever doubt the love she showed for you. She loved you."

Before I know it, another innocent "why?" has burst from my lips. Perhaps it isn't innocent, but I pronounce it the way I always do, without any double meaning, as if I simply want to make a discovery. No. This was the "why" I always annoyed Mama with when she was trying to tell me something. This "why" just wanted to understand what was coming next.

"I don't know," said Nina-hanum, and sighed. "Maybe she knew what you were going through. They worked together, you know. Natasha was a film editor. As far as I know, in Malnikov's last movie, she was in charge of the editing team, but she left that job before it was finished and spent seven months taking care of you."

I don't know what I was going through. This time, the anxious "whys" were spinning right before my eyes.

Nina-hanum squeezed my hand tighter. "She was also in love."

I started to sob.

"I don't remember, Nina-hanum, I'm only guessing, and I feel so sad. My guess is that I came here to find something... But I don't know!" My nose was running, but I didn't want to take my hand away from her. I tucked my face into my shoulder.

"Sweetheart, listen, it's good that you don't remember. You chose a dead-end path. But if you want, I can tell you about Natasha. Natasha was in love with Mikhail Malnikov. Everyone was in love with Malnikov. I would have been, too, if I were younger. He's a man that, when you stand next to him, you feel as if you're behind a stone wall, sturdy and impenetrable. He had such an alluring way of paying attention to everyone around him... Natasha loved him like mad, but she tried to keep her distance. Why? Malnikov had a wife and two children, and he loved them very much. On the day he came to see you, he paid the whole cost of your treatment, and left me more money on top of that, just in case we needed anything, so I wouldn't worry about the expense. The day that I called your mother in to see you, he came again. There were tears in his eyes. He knelt before your mother. He said, 'I wanted to do something good for her, but the opposite happened. If only it had all been up to me...' Your mother is a woman with insight, one of the things I love about her. Do you know what she said? She said, 'Every person has to make their own choice, and that freedom of choice and the things other people choose aren't always what we would like.'"

Nina-hanum may not have said much, but she was untangling the threads. I had rewoven and torn apart those threads many times. Now, after my illness, those threads were tied into tight knots.

My eyes flooding with tears, I ran from one furrow to the next, but all I could see was the white of the cotton. Suddenly, there was darkness: the tractor's shadow. Without thinking, I jumped inside the machine and put my hands on the wheel. Its rattling voice rang out. I wanted that voice to be louder, I wanted it to explode. I wanted everyone to know he had betrayed me. Lied to me. No, he hadn't said anything. Not saying is also a lie. Hiding the truth is a lie. No. No, I can't believe that there was any reason for all that disregard! I don't believe I had been so blind, acted so childishly. What had I been hoping for? He never said that he loved me. He never said... No, he never said anything. So why did I get myself in so deep? Why didn't anyone explain things to me? Why didn't anyone tell me he had a girlfriend, that he loved another woman? Why did I tie my heart so tightly to a man with whom I never talked about a single thing, other than work? We never took the risk of talking about real life... So why am I now so furious at reality? Why am I running? Where am I running to? Now the tractor is at the edge of the sea. I've forgotten where I am. I let go of the wheel, and the land with all its slopes and hollows rolls the tractor right to the water.

This is the only scene preserved in my memory from the last day of shooting. I remember how I came back and saw the people waving at me, and I couldn't hear anything. My ears were blocked, dead. I couldn't hear what Nina-hanum was saying. I squeezed her hand. She stopped talking.

My nostrils caught a familiar scent. My heart beat faster, faster still... I looked in both directions. Nobody. It was the scent that poured from his collar at sunset, by the fire, when he wove his fingers with mine and we kept stepping back, then coming closer. My arms and legs felt weak. I was drunk, enraptured, helpless. The idea that we would have to unlace our fingers so soon and sit down on different sides of the fire and satisfy ourselves with glances was unbearable.

"It doesn't matter, Nina-hanum. What matters is love and the days of joy that we had. I want to see them. Both of them." I don't know why her tears flowed so bitterly when I said that: "Both of them."

She shook her head. "I don't know. If I had known... It's as if I want to see them, too, myself."

It hadn't been more than half an hour since our conversation. I was occupying myself by pacing my room. From one corner to the next. I wanted to be in the endless field, now, running toward the horizon. A powerful-looking man knocked on the door but didn't come in. I had left it half open; I was expecting the head of the archives, whom Nina-hanum had told to come get me. I threw a wool shawl over my shoulders and stepped into the corridor. I gave the stranger my hand to shake, and I thanked him. He led me down the narrow hallway toward the doors and smiled. "I'm happy to see you again."

A cold sweat broke out on my forehead. I tried hard to read, in his gaze, what it was that once connected us. What was that gentle gaze telling me about? A genuine friendship, or something more? Or less? My arms were crossed as usual, my fingers clutching my elbows.

Everyone here knew me. That look! "Right, that's... Yes." Those looks said "yes," and when whispers went with them, I always felt stupid. It's the sensation that you belong here and are also a stranger. Kind people and flashing eyes that wished me well were always following me, and with every door I walked through, I wondered where I had seen them before. That look, those eyes... Until I ran into the next look and the same question all over again. My head was spinning.

It had taken a week for me to receive permission to search the archives of video recordings from the camera in my room. They said, "Nobody ever asked to do anything like this before, and we've never let anyone into the storage room. Except for one time, when we were looking for a thief who was stealing patients' things."

I walked down the hallway. It was dark, and there was an odd smell. No patients. I could have been a prisoner of this hallway. The farther I walked, the darker it got. I remembered the time when I traveled this same route, taking tiny steps, pressing my back against the wall. I was afraid that my shadow would appear and fall at my feet. I was afraid of shadows and darkness. I couldn't budge in my terror, I stood pinned fast to the wall, until somebody appeared and told me, with a smile, that there was no danger. I stopped. The man turned around. His gaze was reassuring. I managed to grab onto an inexplicable trust in him, and embrace it.

We walked through an iron door. It closed behind us with a dull click. This was the basement storage room, the archives. Shelves full of numbered boxes. Each had a sticker with a four-digit numeral.

I looked around. I heard my guide's voice coming from behind a shelf. "This way, please!" He was standing next to a table with a big television monitor hanging over it, and seven or eight smaller screens on the wall nearby. A different image on each screen. A woman sitting. Someone pacing back and forth. An old lady getting ready for bed. The screen on the big television was dark.

There was a box on the table with the number, or the date, 1998. My guide opened the box, pulled out a video cassette the size of a small book, and put it in the player. The light in the room was so blinding I could not easily make out the picture. The man explained in a few sentences how to swap the tapes and rewind them. For a second, he put his hand on my shoulder, and then he walked to the door. On his way out, he gave me one more look, and spun the dial on the light switch. The light in the room dimmed, and the picture grew clearer.

A slight shiver seized my body. I pressed the play button. A black and white image. No, more like gray and yellow. They had recorded the entire first week of my illness and all my visitors for the seven months I had stayed here.

October 10, 1998.

A girl sits on a chair and talks with the table lamp. She lifts it up and puts it down again as if she wants to test its weight. She lifts the lamp and stares hard at its underside. As if she's looking for something. As if she wants to know where it was made.

The lamp suddenly drops from her hands onto the rug, but it goes on glowing. The girl jumps up and sits down on the bed. She looks first at the camera, then at the lamp. This is the same girl who was sitting on the bed in the photograph. But she's hunched over, and her hair is cut short, like a soldier's.

The girl shouts. The lamp goes out. In the dark room, her eyes glow like two small stars. A young woman walks briskly into the room and turns on the lamp. Natasha! It's Natasha. The editor who took her editor's knife to the film of my life, as well...

I put my hand into the box of video cassettes and rifle through them hungrily, like I've found a cache of treasure. I remember how at night, while everyone slept, the director used to turn on the monitor and search for something in the footage we had filmed. When he found the right place, he locked his fingers behind his head and looked long and hard at this discovery. With sound, without sound, with sound but nothing else... I knew that in the minutes of film he was re-examining, something wasn't working.

I used to sit next to him taking in the radiant picture of the field, people's voices, the distant roar of the tractor, and the singing of the women picking cotton. The director used to say, "I can't believe this light. Asian light! Unbridled, unleashed, so free! Wild light that won't ever be tamed!"

But these hospital videos, without light and life, exuded only the feeling of profound oppression. Natasha was right. If I had stayed here, my memory might never have come back, and I would never have breathed in the scent of "Asian" life again.

October 16.

The girl has been lying in bed for a long time without getting up. The door yawns open and Natasha walks in, right on time, down to the minute. The girl does not move. Natasha fiddles with this and that, keeping one eye on the girl.

Natasha reaches for a piece of paper on the table, covered with writing, and starts to read. She lowers her head closer over the page. Closer. The girl on the bed sits up a little and grabs the page from Natasha's hands. Natasha stands up abruptly and grips the back of the chair. The girl hides the paper under her blanket. Natasha sits down again. Soon enough, she says goodbye and leaves.

The girl gets out of bed. As if she has been waiting for Natasha to go. She shuts the door tight. She circles the room and runs a hand over the padded wall, dappled with writing. She mutters to herself.

Just then, Nina Ivanovna stopped by to see me. When she saw the date on the recording, she said, "We wanted to clean the room on that day. Replace the wall coverings. You absolutely refused to let us."

I turned when I heard Nina-hanum's voice. I jumped up and offered her my chair. She sat. "Then, you didn't want to, and now, I don't want to. How often do they bring us an actress from Samarqand, after all?" I loved her hoarse laughter. But I always hated it when she called me an actress.

She patted me on the shoulder. "Dinner's getting cold. Let's go. Everyone is waiting."

"I need a few more minutes."

"How long?"

"Two minutes."

"Then I'll wait here."

"Please, you go ahead, I'll—"

"We'll go together," she says.

I stand up reluctantly. I collect all the papers on the worktable. I reach for the knob, but all of a sudden, somebody walks into the hospital room. Natasha again. She sits next to the bed and lifts the covers slightly away from the girl's face as she lies there.

Nina-hanum puts her hand on my shoulder. "Let's go." She seems to know that if I don't go with her, I'll forget about dinner and will go hungry until tomorrow.

The hospital cafeteria was full of men and women, clearly waiting for me. When they saw us, they all stood up at once, raising their glasses. This was the hospital's feast to celebrate my return and my recovery. Twenty or thirty people, nodding to me, and shouting a toast: "To your health, Mahtab!" There were two empty chairs. Nina Ivanovna and I took those chairs and a glass of vodka apiece. "To your health!" I heard the short ring of the clinking glasses. The people brought the glasses to their faces, like oxygen masks, and emptied them.

The first time I inhaled cigarette smoke, there was the same taxing sensation: a burning shock wave filled my mouth and burst to the outside. But the shock wave from the vodka shot inside, scorching everything in its path. That wasn't my first time drinking vodka. But it was my first time downing two hundred grams at once.

"Astounding bitterness that brings sweetness in the end," wrote Natasha. "I know it's hard for you, but please believe the day will come when you will say, 'It's good that this is the way everything happened.'" Mama loved what she wrote next: "We Russians rejoice in the present and prepare for troubles tomorrow, but you Eastern people spend the present day in troubles and torments, in hopes of rejoicing tomorrow. I'm not saying which one is better; I'm saying that you will achieve everything you're striving for."

The girl's lethargy and indifference whenever Natasha was there probably troubled her. I tell myself that if I were in her place, I'd grab that girl and physically force her out of bed. But Natasha just sits calmly and writes a note at the bottom of each page that is strewn across the table. Like a teacher grading her students' homework.

There are flowers in the pot, and they look happier than the girl. Natasha walks to the window and looks outside.

I don't know when that supper ended or what I ended up saying to the men and women gathered around me. But I like to imagine I was lively and cheerful, and eternally grateful to them for caring for me all that time and returning me safely to the land of my mothers.

Nina Ivanovna walked around the room, touching the writing on the walls, now bowing her head, now stretching her neck, getting lost in the florid chain of words. She had stopped by to give me a letter from Natasha. I began reading it out loud.

Nina-hanum sat on my bed and looked at me, a glass in her hand. Absorbed in my reading, I almost didn't notice she was there.

Mahtab, darling! I'm writing all this because I'm confident it will no longer cause you pain. What happened to you could have happened to me. When you're next to the fire, the thing you should be most careful of is not getting burned.

That's a fire I warmed myself next to for a very long time... I loved Mikhail. Exactly like you did. Maybe love isn't the right word... I found refuge in his authenticity, his simplicity. When I decided to go and see who she was—this girl who had so captured his attention—my heart was full of hatred. I consider myself guilty. What happened was my fault. But now that I've heard news of your recovery and found my peace, I want to congratulate you.

We might never see each other again. You might not remember me, or forget me. But please know that you were my salvation. I'm sending you your writings. You should have them.

Say hello to your mother for me. Nina Ivanovna has some of your things—I'm sure she'll send them to you.

That was the end of the letter, but I couldn't bring myself to lift my head. Nina-hanum put her hand on my shoulder. "I have the money Malnikov left for you, and he and I signed an agreement that we'd keep this room the way it is, as much as possible. He wanted to use it for a film sometime."

When Nina Ivanovna handed me her handkerchief, her own eyes were red, too. The questions burst out of me. "Where? Do you know?"

She looked me in the eye. She patted my shoulder. "Now, now. It's too soon for you. This is all very upsetting—"

"Where? Do you know?"

She shook her head and handed me my glass.

Neither she nor I uttered any names. Did I mean Mikhail or Natasha? I didn't know. As hard as I searched for Natasha, Mikhail's tracks were always emerging on the surface. Mikhail was the link connecting me with Natasha.

☙ ❧

It was late. I walked out of the basement storage room. Standing tall, I walked all the way down the corridor and opened the door to my room. There were papers piled everywhere. Thank God, they had honored my request and hadn't cleaned up my room. Again I sat down at the table, picked up a pile of pages, and tossed them in the wastebasket.

I was tired of reading all these fragments, with no beginning or end in sight. A sharp pain kept nagging me, from my neck to the small of my back. I eased myself down onto the bed.

I don't know how long I sat on that grim hospital cot in that dark, cramped room. The idea of leaving the hospital had seemed impossible. If Natasha hadn't been so insistent, I probably never would have left here. I would have contented myself with the cold suns staring from the walls. Natasha had summoned Mama and handed me over to her. She put my suitcase onto the baggage rack in the train compartment and said, "Say hello to the Asian sun."

I walked out, planning to get myself some tea or coffee and then come sit down at the table again. I wanted to find a trace of Natasha in this riddle of notes.

There was a stranger in the hallway. He introduced himself: Natasha's father. He must have seen the joy in my eyes because he hurried to say, "Unfortunately, I don't have any good news for you. Natasha left long ago, and her mother and I don't know where she is."

He had come to invite me to dinner. I recognized his old Volga. Natasha had driven that car to the hospital, and sometimes she took me for drives around the city. She loved the beautiful, harsh Moscow nights, the darkness and the mischievous lights, winking alluringly. It was as if Natasha and I were the only ones not in a hurry, the only ones who didn't notice that we were slowing down all the other cars on the road and their nervous drivers. For us, all was calm. In the quiet of our long nighttime drives, when neither one of us said a word, we nevertheless heard everything.

Natasha's father didn't say much either. It seemed that not even curiosity was stirring inside him—why had my memory suddenly returned? Why had I come back here and moved in to the hospital? No, he didn't ask any questions. I looked out the window without speaking all the way to his house. That silence might have been broken once or twice, but then the curtain fell between us again.

I had almost never seen the streets of Moscow free of snow. Every time I had come to this city, the snow had been rioting. It was a cold, white riot, in which even the star at the top of the Kremlin couldn't warm a soul. Mama had come here frequently for work. She had a lot of friends in Moscow. But why, then, was there no mention of Moscow in her diary? Why hadn't her memories ever left the confines of the cotton field?

Mama had seen so many different automobiles, she'd driven so many of them and ridden in so many others, but why did she always write about the old kolkhoz tractor? Moscow was a city of questions, not the answers that I kept hoping to find. Mama had also been full of questions without answers when she wrote.

I sat next to the driver to make him drive faster to the edge of the field, toward the canal, under the tree. When you squeeze shut your bleeding nose, and lift your head and look up, everything looks different. I suddenly wondered how these people's lives looked to the tractor. That thought held me in its grip for a long time.

Everything around suddenly changed in volume, in length, in distance. Sometimes a feeling like that creeps into my brain and I feel empty. Maybe what is precious to me seems ordinary to other people.

In ten minutes, maybe even less, we had put some distance between ourselves and the women weeding. The tractor's life moved at a quicker pace than ours. If I had walked this far, it would have taken three hours tramping under the hot sun, bending down to the ground, from time to time, to tear out a weed, as was my habit—and there was a real risk that I wouldn't make it to the edge of the field before sunset.

I sat down at the stream and thought about speed. The speed of the blood flowing from your nose, for instance. If it doesn't stop, you might be all out of blood in an hour. Or about how to overcome distance without moving. How can you work the earth and reap the harvest without ever touching a hoe? How can you rip up the wild weeds without ever bending over? Or sit in the shade and drink a cup of cool doogh, like our women, with the rhythms of life in no way disrupted.

The tractor moved quicker than we women did. A train was faster than a tractor, and an airplane was faster than any of us. I had less and less faith in human legs. On foot, you can't take full advantage of the opportunities. You always necessarily miss one.

When my thoughts overwhelmed me, I fell ill and lost my faith in work and in life. Now I can't shake the thought of the lonely tractor in the steppe, the thought of its orphanhood. Why is something that does so much good so alone? We encounter good so rarely, or else we never encounter it at all. Sometimes I wonder what would need to be done to make women able to work like the tractor.

I looked out the windows of the car. At each intersection, I turned and peered in a new direction. I thought I saw Natasha, walking slowly, head tucked down into the collar of her coat. My breath fogged the window. I felt something unexplainable.

When Natasha's mother finally opened the door, the warmth of her gaze cracked the ice in my heart. That ice had been growing thicker all the way here from the hospital.

This kind woman knew all about me. She tells me that every day, when Natasha came home from the hospital, she used to talk about how I was feeling, about what I could remember, and sometimes Natasha would even read her my notes.

Every Russian home, with its monotone wallpaper, has a similar atmosphere. The old yellow paper on the walls, marked by the outlines of whatever piece of furniture used to be there. Natasha left the same kind of mark on the wall of my consciousness.

The dream of seeing her daughter again is what keeps Natasha's mother going. How many days and nights has that same dream held me in its grip! The days and nights when I search for Natasha among my scraps of writing, whether made in a haze or in my right mind, among the meters of film in the hospital archives, between the glances of friends and strangers. I'm looking for the girl who cared for me for seven months, so I could regain my memory; then once I regained it, she disappeared.

Natasha's mother brought in a family photo album and put it on the table. The table was sticky, and every time I lifted my arm off its surface, I heard a wet sucking sound. The oilcloth was old and sliced through in places, decorated with flowers, their jaws gaping wide.

The woman told me about Natasha's childhood and adolescence. When her story approached the time when I appeared in her daughter's life, she abruptly changed the subject. "How is Aftab these days? Doing well? What is she up to?"

"Yes, she's fine. She says hello. She wanted to send you some watermelons, but decided not to risk it. They confiscate things like that on the railroad. There have been passengers who had every inch of their bags searched at the Kazakh border, and they took all the fruit they had and threw it off the train. Everything's gotten stricter lately, I hear."

"Yes, they say on the news that corruption is up at the border."

"It's always been like that," I say.

"No, in Soviet times it was fine," she says.

"That could be."

My eyes dart around the apartment. I'm looking for traces of Natasha. She is nothing like either her mother or her father.

The sound engineer wasn't a talkative guy. I didn't think he would remember me or want to see me. Probably he was thinking about Natasha his whole journey over the snowy sidewalk. Every time he lifted a foot off the cold Moscow ground, he remembered her, and remembering those sweet summer days, he planted that foot on the ground again. Natasha's mother had told me, "The sound engineer is in love with Natasha, and sometimes he stops by to visit me. He comes, smokes a cigarette, and disappears again." That's the kind of person he is. He used to come up to me back in the cotton field, too, and sit down, and he could tell if I was angry or upset just by a quick touch of my hand or shoulder. Then he would walk away. He infused us all with his sense of calm, and his eyes were always saying that everything is more or less shit and we shouldn't take it seriously.

This time, when he plodded over and sat down, I sensed he could no longer understand so much with one small move. I could not figure out what I could do to make him lift his head and look me in the eye. What could I do to ease that weight around his temples? What could I do to drag him out from his own worries and into the light?

He had come to smoke a pile of cigarettes, and to tell me, as he left, "You had a chance, back then, to dump your whole memory in the canal and get free."

We were sitting in a sidewalk café, and the air was heavy with the aroma of the steaming samsas on the table. We hadn't touched the food. We put down our cigarettes, we lifted our glasses; we put down our glasses and lifted our cigarettes. The café's windows were fogged over on the inside. In the two hours we sat there facing one another, he never mentioned Natasha's name, nor Mikhail's. Sometimes the tobacco smoke wrapped around his shoulders, sometimes mine. He told me, "The film was a bust. It didn't turn out the way we wanted it to. They hacked it to pieces—you could see the knife marks. They sliced out the most amazing scenes, but it's the crew's hearts that bled." He bit his lip to keep from swearing.

The August sun knew no mercy. The trailer was no longer of any use as a refuge from the torture the sun beat down on us. Closing its metal door was like shutting yourself in a tanur to bake, multiplying the heat inside by ten. Mama was not tolerating it well, and her heart rate was going inexorably up. Finally she had to go and leave the film crew to their own devices.

Everyone had abandoned their tents and started hiding under the trees. Half undressed, we swam in the canal and dried off right there, instantly, on the breezy steppe. I was wearing a blouse I had cut the sleeves off to fight the heat, and cutoff shorts as well, and I was talking with the sound engineer while I peeled an apple. The peel dangled in spiral rings, then broke off and fell in my lap.

Mikhail walked over, in his straw hat and dark sunglasses.

"Hi."

There were his thin, hairy knees, directly before me. Paying him no attention, I went on demonstratively peeling my apple. He plopped down next to us, took a ribbon of apple peel from my lap, and lifted it to the sky. This time, I looked at him, and I knew his mouth would be open. He loved doing that: holding food above his head, and letting it drop right into his mouth. His lips moved in circles, like a camel's.

He lay down, propped up on one elbow. I could hear him chewing. I took a bite of my peeled apple. He sat up a little and reached out his hands, palms up. I took another bite. His hands remained there, hanging in the air.

The sound engineer was occupied with his own worries, as if he were the only one there. This time, it was my chewing that broke the silence.

I was angry at Mikhail. I couldn't forget the sharp words he had let fly at me while we were filming.

"No, no, no. How many times do I have to tell you? Sweetheart, listen." He went and grabbed one of the local girls by the hand and ran up to me, dragging her with him. "A woman who picks cotton has hands like this. Just like this. See?" I looked at her hands, crisscrossed with wrinkles, skin burnt black by the sun. There were cuts visible here and there that Mikhail took pains to point out. Annoyed, I flung my cloth sack of cotton to the ground.

My hands were freshly washed, the filth carefully pried out from under my fingernails.

"How many times do I have to say this? Don't touch your makeup! No touching!"

I hid my fingernails guiltily and mumbled, "But I was having lunch."

He yelled back, angrier than before. "Whatever the hell you're doing, don't touch your makeup!"

In a fit of fury, I bent down, scooped up a handful of earth, and threw it into my own face. "Is this good? How's this for makeup?!" Everyone around burst out laughing. I ran out of there. I didn't know which direction I was running. I always ran when I was angry or hurt. West, east, south—I didn't know. All I knew was that running made it better. The earth caressed me with its firmness and the weight it conveyed, and the pain, too, of the tiny sharp parts of it that stuck through my shoes. Those sensations reached my brain, and I forgot the pain in my soul.

I was tired of this mannish swamp-colored military uniform from Soviet times. I missed the short, light outfits the local women wore. Our traditional clothing came in a thousand colors. The breeze could slip inside it in a single gust, and run out the other side, carrying the heat of your body with it.

I crossed my arms tightly and headed toward home. "Hey! Where are you going? Stop! I'm talking to you! This is all I need... I don't have time to coddle you!"

That wasn't the first time I walked off the set. Everyone knew I would be back. For Mama's sake, for whom this movie was the most important thing in the world, and who had never been happier than she was now. She observed the whole filming process and every single scene. This film was like a holiday for her. And to be sure, she also felt a deep pride for my acting in it.

Every time I got upset at Mikhail's meanness, Mama shored me up, restored my confidence. That day Mama wasn't there, and the sound engineer followed me instead. He didn't say anything about what had happened. He just sat down next to me and took out some apples. My favorite kind, the sweet white ones.

But then the director shows up. He probably wants me to stop being angry. I take two bites from that apple and stand up. His hands are still outstretched. Moving away from him, I feel I've left my heart in those hands... And my heart was saying, "No! Don't go. Sit down. He's here to ask you to forgive him, again." But my pride refused. "No! Why does he do it? Yell at me in front of everyone, and then one little apology, and everything is fine?"

I opened the door to the trailer and walked in, even though I knew I might die of the heat inside. It was the only place where I could hide from all those eyes. I took out Mama's diary and used it to fan my chest and armpits. There was a knock at the door. I didn't respond. I knew it was him. I knew that when he told me, "Everyone's here, we're starting," without leaving me any time for makeup, he did it on purpose, so that he'd have a reason to chew me out later.

Everyone knew it. His nagging was becoming a cliché. But when I retreated, he advanced. When I moved toward him, he purposefully moved away. Without waiting for me to answer, Mikhail came into the trailer. I glared at him. He took one more step inside and sat down in the doorway. "They say there's a girl getting cooked in a tanur over here. I've come to eat her up." He had such a medieval sense of humor. If only I didn't feel anything for him—then I could hit him over the head with something heavy and shove him out of my trailer. I gathered all my strength and hit him with a firm look instead. It dissolved in his gentle grin. He always came, sent that soft look into my eyes, and left again. And that look of his made me putty in his hands. It was a look that spread throughout my body, so much so that it surfaced in my own eyes and finally came to rest there, cozy and warm. A look that now seemed to belong to me.

My watch has left an imprint on my forehead. I look at the door. Closed. I don't know when I fell asleep. I had put my head down on my arms and drifted off, right here in this basement storage room.

The videocassette had ejected itself from the player. Nothing but monotonous scenes, no movement, sleep-inducing. But this was the best way to see that foggy, forgotten time, when my only occupation had been staring at the suns scratched into the padded hospital walls. A picture that never leaves the camera's lens, like a sign or a symbol.

I take one of the pages that are strewn on the table and read it.

I don't know how many days I've been here in this tiny room. I sleep and don't have the strength to get up. If only they didn't make me get up... I really can't. My head spins when I lift it off the pillow. Sometimes the ceiling whirls so much it makes me sick. I'm waiting for someone to come and relieve me of this acidic wave of vomit before it erupts from me again. When I see the nurse scowl like that, I wish I were dead...

Natasha's insistence that I have to remember everything has robbed me of my equanimity. It's as if she knows something about my life, my very soul, that I don't know myself. Today she brought a pile of videos and photos. I looked at the pictures. A man on top of a truck, behind a movie camera. His face looked familiar. But I didn't remember anything. Natasha started to cry. I don't know why she's always crying.

She says that man is sick, too. Why should I care? Am I supposed to keep track of all the sick people now? "Hey, Doctor, I think Natasha is sick, too. Every day when she comes in, she asks me what my name is." The doctor goes on about her business as if I don't exist. As if I'm not here, as if nobody is here. I look at the half-open door: "Doctor? Natasha is sick." This time the doctor tears her eyes away from her notebook and lifts her head. I go back to the table and start to write. I write a title. I have to tell the doctor. It was as if I needed to write to work it all out.

Hello, Miss? Every morning you read my notes. Could you examine Natasha? I think she's sick. For several days now, she's been showing me my own photograph and saying, "This is your mama."

I don't trust Natasha, Doctor. Could you keep her out of my room from now on? She keeps calling me Shura. I don't know why. There must be something wrong with her. She scares me.

I tear myself away from the tiny, disorganized notes and look at the screen. I feel sorry for Natasha. Sorry for all the times she puts her head on my shoulder and smiles, and says, "That girl is named Aftab..." Then she points at her stomach, and says, "That girl is your mama." She rubs her face in my hair like a cat. A moan bursts in her throat and shards of it escape to the outside.

The words slip gently from her mouth, and sometimes they melt there. That has never happened to me. My tongue is so clumsy and such a mismatch with my teeth that my words always get ground to a pulp, and sometimes I can even hear the crack when they break.

"Stop! Stop!" Clapping his hands, the director sends everyone's concentration scattering like so many pigeons. "Listen! How many times do I have to tell you? Don't maim your words! Let them speak freely! OK? All right, again, let's go!"

I had to run through the rain and try to get everyone back. The old women and the children, loads of cotton on their shoulders, were all walking to the scales. They were running. Everyone was getting soaked with rain. Every drop made the cotton heavier. The scale man refused to put the damp cotton on the scales, but the people didn't want to drop what they carried in the middle of the field. It was my responsibility to make everyone stop, make them stay where they were and wait for the rain to go away, then get back to work. And it was my job to assign each person a row early in the morning, and at the end of the day each of them was supposed to hand back their row nice and clean and bring the cotton they had picked to the scales. Until every row was harvested, I didn't let them into the next plot. Snow, rain, it made no difference: we had rules to obey.

I ran and thought about what Mama had written. Mama, when she ran, had thought about why the people didn't drop the cotton they had picked. Why didn't they run away? Why did they sit there in the rain? Because she told them to? Or were they actually afraid of losing the loads they bore? If they were afraid, then of what? Damp cotton? Catching cold? No. The people weren't afraid. The people didn't know that they had a choice.

I ran and ran through the rain. Even the director shouting "Wait, wait!" couldn't stop me. I ran for the people who weren't allowed to run and weren't allowed to stay in the rain.

I ran in order to see what the people saw, and what the director saw. I ran, and he watched the rain.

The rain smacked the cotton in the face, and the sunset tossed a velvet shawl over the shoulders of the steppe.

I strained to make out the words on one of my scraps of writing from when I was ill, and I copied it neatly into my notebook.

Until today, for me, there have never been any rules or laws, and I lived the way my heart told me to. You Russians made up artificial rules for everything.

When Natasha read that, she cheered up. "So you know that we're Russians, and you're not? Tell me, Shura, tell me! You must have remembered something!"

"My name's not Shura. My name is Aftab. Aftab!" And I angrily grabbed the old photos away from her. I spend a long time—how long, I don't know—looking at one of them. A girl running toward the sunset.

"As long as there's a cotton field, it's nice to keep running." Natasha stands up and glances at the clock. "I need to get going. But promise me you'll write down everything you remember." She walks to the door, sees her reflection in the mirror, and comes back. "But yesterday... Did you forget Shura from yesterday?"

I give her a surprised look. "Shura?"

Last night I ran out of paper again, and I wrote on the sheet, the pillow, the mattress—everything I could get my hands on. But the fat woman gathered it all up and took it away.

I don't know what time it is or how many videotapes I've watched. This one is almost over. Nothing out of the ordinary is happening in the room, just the same scenes repeating themselves. The girl spends hours sleeping, and hours writing on the walls and door.

I rifle through the pages I've arranged on the table, trying to sort out which one was written on which day. When the girl gets tired of writing, she burrows under the blanket and lies motionless. I don't know how many times I've re-read these notes. Maybe I'm looking for a sign, or a hint as to where Natasha might be.

The fat woman came into the room, but I seemed to have passed out from all my sleepless nights and didn't wake up. The woman sat next to the wood-framed bed. She put her hands over her face and wept. Just sat there, calm as you please, weeping. Then she stood up, rolled the girl closer to the wall, pulled the sheet covered with writing out from under her, and replaced it with a clean one. She collected the torn scraps of paper that were scattered around the room and piled them neatly on the table. She looked under the bed and froze, then dropped to one knee on the rug. Again she started to cry. What was under there? The camera angle didn't let me see.

Today Natasha came with a handsomely dressed man. She put two packs of white paper on the table, along with a few ballpoint pens. She gathered up all the books, magazines, and newspapers she had brought me recently. The handsomely dressed man seemed to have come to keep watch over her. He didn't say anything, just quietly observed her every move.

Natasha was wearing a collarless dress. When she bent over and stood up again, her white breasts trembled and swayed, as if they wanted to escape, dive right off her thin frame. Her breasts were making such an effort that anybody would have rushed to help them, your hands lift toward them of their own accord, but again and again they fall. The man sat there silently, never taking his eyes off Natasha. He might have been crazy. He looked riveted to something that wasn't there.

But his face was so familiar... I look more closely. It's him! So all that time, he was coming to visit me, as Natasha's escort! And all that time, he knew where I was! Where is he now? With Natasha, probably. They had plenty of time to cry their eyes out over my misfortune, or laugh, or get used to it, or get tired of it and move away. And leave the sick girl with amnesia to muddle through herself. I look at that girl: She's asleep in the bed like a small wild animal, cute, but pitiful.

I stand up. Now I understand why Natasha was so confident, why she insisted that I wasn't who I thought I was. She said that the film script and Mama's diary full of memories had gotten crossed in my brain. Maybe. But why, when I read Mama's writing, do I relive everything with my whole being? As if it happened to me?

One hot summer day, when the sun was at its peak and the local women and I were hoeing in the field—ripping out the "stranger grass," as we called the weeds, by the roots—my nose started to bleed. Mama came up, horrified. "I asked you to hoe the weeds, not tear out the young cotton plants that worked so hard to sprout!" From that day on, I knew what cotton could do. I was six years old when Mama told me, "Never kill a young cotton plant. The cotton will take its revenge." Mama always laughed when I called it "our grass" instead of "cotton." When Mama laughed, her bosom stood still, as if she didn't have breasts at all. As if she had given them away. As if she had no need of two round white breasts which were always flopping side to side or billowing outward. As if the stern hand of fate had hoed out her breasts as well.

Using the hoe didn't come naturally to me. I felt sorry for the pretty wild plants, and I left them alone. A young shoot of cotton had a narrow green waist and a crown of four bright green leaves. That was the only way I could tell cotton from anything else. Later I learned some of them have a group of just two or three leaves, but that was rare. I only recognized the four-leaf cotton plant, and I yanked out all the other specimens by the roots and tore off their heads. I was basically hopeless at weeding. That day, when the shoots of cotton cut down before their time put their curse on me and my nose bled, I looked at the field with new eyes. Mama lifted me up and handed me to the kolkhoz driver, and for the second time in my life, I sat in the cab of the tractor, the same one that had driven me home as a newborn. The seat was so high up that the rows of young cotton looked like one unbroken line, stretching to the very edge of the field. The sight of thirty or forty women, bent over permanently in the endless field, was frightening. Like a throng of ants dragging a spikelet of wheat from a heap of grass. I hadn't been carrying a sack I could use to gather the weeds I picked. Usually Mama, walking behind me, picked them up, using her hands that, in the freshness of her youth, had caressed the heads and faces of every branch of every cotton plant, leaving that freshness and youth behind.

The next day, I told the kolkhoz chairman that I was tired of bringing water to all those women. Why didn't they all strap a canteen to their belts and take a drink whenever they felt like it, instead of calling me over all the time? The chairman turned to me and said, "First of all, where am I supposed to get so many belts and canteens? And second of all, if we do that, you'll be unemployed." I say, "I'll be the tractor driver's apprentice!" He says, "First you spend a good year being the water carrier's apprentice. Then you can celebrate."

Our water carrier is a crippled young man who rides an old mule. He struggles to fill two barrels of water from the well and then spends half a day riding back. He delivers water once each day. If you're dying of thirst at the start of the day, or the end of the day, too bad for you. Many times, it's true, I carried a bucket of water all the way to the cemetery and on to the middle of the collective farm for the sake of some pregnant woman.

The apple and peach trees that grow in the cemetery are such a pleasant sight! But where we live, nobody touches their sweet fruit. They say their ruddiness comes from our own dearly departed. Many times it's happened that hunger and thirst drove me to reach for an apple, and a couple times I even took a bite, but my stomach revolted, and I could never keep it down. Just the feeling that your mouth is full of the blood and bones of your grandmother, lying dead in that cemetery, can make you sick. They take that fruit to the outdoor market and turn it into money, and other people eat it. We always hold our hands open in prayer and give thanks for the bountiful harvest of the cemetery orchard. The district's most talented gardener is buried there, too, and they say that at night he rises from his grave and tends to the trees.

I don't believe a word of it, needless to say. I've never believed those silly fairy tales. But even if I did believe them, I wouldn't be scared. My bibi used to say that the spirit of the earth is more powerful than the spirits of all human beings put together. While the spirit of the earth is with you, you're safe. I seemed to believe I was a child of the steppe, a child of the earth. Many people thought I would be the future chairman of the kolkhoz.

I wasn't afraid of being the chairman. The kolkhoz chairman was the only person who knew where all this hard work by men and women went to, year after year.

Sometimes, as part of my job as deputy chairman, I had to report women or girls who spent too much time sitting down during working hours, or made excuses not to work. The women got mad at me when I reported them to the chairman. I understand the chairman better. He says, "If one woman sits down to rest, ten percent of the work stops. If everyone sits down to rest together, all the work stops." I would do anything to keep the rules of the land from being broken.

It's a good thing I'm a girl and, sooner or later, like Mama, I'll feel the pulse of the earth and take on unlimited responsibility for this whole unceasing process, all the work. I think I understand that where there is land, there is cotton, and where there is cotton, women have work to do. Poor, poor men... They have to sit and wait till night falls and the women come home from the fields, eat some bread, and fall asleep. Then the stronger sex can go, their minds calm and their axes in hand, and make a run on the collective farm's water supply to steal a little for their own small gardens and yards.

Ivan dragged a fat bundle of weeds out from the tractor's cab, squatted down next to me, and put the soft bundle under my head. My nose went hot again, and the thick, viscous blood crept like a caterpillar down from my brain. Then he pulled the bundle out from under my head and I was back lying flat on the earth, face to the sky.

The sun must be a man. It keeps its distance from the earth and contemplates us from above. Every time I lie on my back like this, peeking under the trees' skirts, the sun touches their sides, their ears, their waists, he wants to tickle them everywhere, and he never gets enough of it.

Mama says that Aftab is a girl's name. I argue, "But everything about the sun's behavior is so masculine!"

Mama asks, "What behavior?"

"It's completely merciless, it burns until it runs out of strength, and all it does is watch and watch! Just like the chairman."

"You have a point about the chairman," Mama says, and laughs.

"Plus," I say, "the girls run away from the sun and hide their faces, like a man might see them."

"They're worried their skin will burn. They're afraid of looking old." Mama sighs.

I look at Ivan's hands. They're not as white as they used to be. But when he takes off his gray undershirt, everyone immediately remembers how white-skinned he is. The women were always forcing more color on him: "Look at you, white as cotton! Come and get in my little sack!" He would stare at each of them in turn, embarrassed, as if wondering, "Is it true? Are you serious? Should I believe you?" But the women rolled on the ground with laughter. Now I'm sure they were jealous that I was sitting here alone with him. Not quite: he was sitting, and I was stretched out on the ground next to him.

I look at his hands. Why doesn't he know how to do the work I know so well? And why don't I know his work? In my lifetime, I have seen one tractor and one tractor driver: this Ivan on his red steel stallion, which he actually pats right on its big wheel, murmuring words of affection.

I remember how the kolkhoz chairman whipped women around their knees, asking, "When are you going to turn into a human being?"

I knew very well the process of making a human being out of a woman. But the women thought I didn't understand when they said, "Well, has so-and-so become human?"

A woman who wanted to become human worked quietly all day, occasionally making eyes at the chairman, who plodded heavily toward her with his thin willow switch in his hands. Her gaze full of tenderness, she would try to soften the chairman's steps and put a little more hope in his burning heart, until the other women, still working, moved away from the two of them. Then there was a quick exchange of gestures. When dusk began to fall, the women all lifted their bundles full of weeds at once: first one jerk to lift those bundles to their knees, a second jerk onto their stomachs, and a third onto their heads. Then they walked off toward the buildings. But the one who wanted to become human always got completely tired out, and she let her heavy bundle (if she had one) fall to the ground, and told her friends, "You go on ahead, I'll just catch my breath." Everyone could see right through that remark.

For a while, that was as much as I ever observed of the humanization process. Mama and I always went home. But one time, I took advantage of—or, really, abused—some commotion among the livestock (the herds always returned from pasture at the same time as the women), and I picked up a stick and ran to help a woman whose bundle a cow intended to eat. The woman was carrying the bundle of weeds on her head, holding it tight with both hands, and she couldn't fight off the animal. I chased the cow away, and then I hid where Mama couldn't see me. I was burning with the desire to know what happens to a woman who decides to go through the humanization process with the chairman.

She sat and waited until the rest of the weeders, along with the cattle herd, were out of sight. There came the chairman, on the other side of the canal, and the woman rolled up her pants and waded across to him. I kept low to the ground, hidden in the grass that grows by the water. I wanted to get up and run away, but a strange curiosity seemed to have pinned me to the earth. I listened to them talking. They had swapped places, and were playing exactly the opposite roles they both played during the workday: Now the woman held a thin branch in her hands, and now *she* was lashing *him* lightly across the shoulders and arms, laughing coquettishly, and asking, "Well? What makes you the master?"

With each strike of the branch, the chairman seemed to come more to life, inflamed, and he moved closer and closer to her. Suddenly he grabbed her in his embrace and they both fell to the ground. Now it was pitch dark, but the woman's laughter seemed to create a halo of light around the two of them. I saw that the woman was safe, and the process of humanization was not that terrible or complicated. I wasn't worried about either of them. The ease with which they rolled around in the grass in each other's arms made it clear that they were both equally happy with how things were going.

In the cotton field, there have been many, many times I've seen women crying about how they've laughed, and laughing at how they've cried. Just as the rain makes the earth blossom.

This time, Natasha had put on eye liner, and I don't know if it was because of that or some other reason that I had trouble recognizing her face. But before she introduced herself for the one thousandth time, I raised a hand and spoke. "Your name is Natasha. But I don't know why you can't leave me alone and have to put in an appearance even on New Year's Eve." When she put her car key down on the table as she always did, I got swept away, off into the world I was searching for. The world I didn't see around me, the world I had to assemble from the fragments between long, chaotic dreams. All because of Natasha. Here was a young woman whose only interest was in restoring my lost memory. Sometimes I wanted to grab Natasha by the arm and say, "Maybe I never had a past. Maybe I don't have anything to remember." But that car key of hers, lying on the table, tossed a stone at me and turned all my thoughts upside down. The key hung from a chain with an old yellow city bus on a thin blue square for a pendant.

I asked Natasha, "Could you bring me a clean pillowcase and sheet by Monday?"

She was surprised. "Why?"

I showed her the bedsheets, full of writing, which I had stashed under my bed. "I don't want them to wash these. I want to keep them."

Natasha walked over and gave me a firm hug. "Your passion for writing is just amazing! I adore you for it." She kissed my head and face.

Something deep inside my heart wanted to say, "But who *are* you, hanum?" I stopped myself in time. I quickly recalled that Natasha was my only friend. She was the only person around here who knew I existed.

Natasha promised to bring me paper and a clean sheet and pillowcase. She was in a hurry, but she still sat down next to me and read attentively what was written on the fabric. That's something I never liked to do. I don't like to read, especially things I wrote myself.

"We all have a past. We have all planted the seeds of our own future in the back alleys of the past."

Natasha confused me even more with those words. Her presence was not helping to restore my memory at all. But when she was near, my fears seemed smaller. My nightmares seemed farther away. She was the only person who spoke honestly with me, generous with both her time and her words. She was the only one who could tolerate me. Natasha said, "The light of the past is in your face and your eyes. It's a light that nobody can take away." I couldn't take my eyes off that blue rectangle on her key chain. There I saw a light that, like sunlight, carried me away to the past, and it had a story to tell me. But who could say if that was my past, or my mother's?

I waited excitedly for the last day of school, so I could finally become a tractor driver and spend morning to night, night to morning, riding its roar across the endless cotton fields. I'd be the earth's mistress, holding all the people's lives in my hands. I had always wanted to occupy the very top position, and the only job where there could be no competition was that unique profession, the driver of the only tractor on the kolkhoz.

The night before, my father had called me to the dinner table and told me, in his most serious tone of voice, that the next day I'd pick up my high school diploma and go with him into the city. I would need to study hard and pull myself out of this muck. What he meant is that I would never become a tractor driver. He was always against my dreams.

Papa wanted me to become a school principal. Of all the different arts and trades, working as a school principal seemed the very least interesting option. Why would anyone want to stand sentry at the school doors first thing in the morning? And then go and shove students' noses into their notebooks and textbooks as they sat at their desks, chase them around the field, begging and threatening them with expulsion? Wasn't that a waste of time? I'd rather be a step above all that and work directly with the people in the field. The school principal is subordinate to the kolkhoz chairman, and when the bosses say they need a workforce of fifty or a hundred units, the principal has no right to send forty-nine or ninety-nine people to the field. In the end, my father and I just could not agree.

Work at the school? Where nobody had any inclination to learn a thing, where the library had been chewed over completely by mice, and the rest of the books had been destroyed last summer because there was a picture of Lenin or the Russian abbreviation CCCP on some page? No, the school principal was the unhappiest person in the whole village! He spent all day chasing restless children to their lessons, punishing them or even the teachers, who rebelled against their students' behavior and often simply refused to come back to work. It would be easier for them to sell fruit from their yards at the market and live off of that. Obviously, commerce brought in more money than teaching.

I thought to myself that at least cotton always stays in its place, and when you arrive, everything is there waiting for you; through all times and all eras, it keeps holding up its head, that same white color, in the same field, on the same land, and the sowing and the harvesting always go the same way. There's no need to burn it or destroy it or dye it if there's a change in the political regime. It's like cotton is some paragon of truth, never losing courage before snow and rain. I told my father, "If being a tractor driver isn't what fate delivers to me, I'll be the kolkhoz chairman."

He looked at me with sympathy. "A trade doesn't fall down on you from above. You need to search it out, pursue it, and make it yours." I say, "I've considered driving to be 'mine' for years and years, but now I see you're opposed to it." He says, "I'm not opposed. I'm just sure that you can find yourself something better."

With no further discussion, the next day I rode with my father to the university. That was the first time I ever saw a university. A big building like a nest, which everyone walked into holding their heads high like self-important idiots. The only person displeased to be stepping over this sacred threshold seemed to be me.

I felt as if I were split in two: one half of me remained back with the tractor, and the other stood here, among these handsomely dressed young people celebrating their admittance.

I felt sorry for them all. I don't know why. "Probably," I thought to myself, "they don't know yet that the university has no library, that all the books have been burned and they're waiting for new ones to be written and printed, and if the political system changes again, those new books will be burned, too, and there won't be any until they write new ones..." These games were repulsive to me, and only driving the tractor seemed a noble pursuit. That tractor was alone in the field, proudly standing tall, where no policy's destructive hand could ever touch it.

My enrollment in the university cost my family ten sheep. So what? Why should I care? I didn't want to be there at all, but my parents made me, and I didn't feel the slightest bit guilty. On the contrary, I was glad that my time there was costing them dearly. Let them see the result of their despotism, I thought.

I slept through my five years as a university student. Aside from sleeping, and going out to the cotton fields, I don't remember anything much from those times. Out of pique, I didn't even go to visit my parents during the summer. The only thing I liked during my student years was cotton harvesting season. That was work I knew how to do and loved. But it did make me sad to see a tractor in a field when nobody would let me drive it. They simply couldn't believe that I knew how, and even if I did know how, they wouldn't have trusted the tractor to me.

There it stood, looming like a holy phantom, its head held high in the endless cotton field so that its crown was in the heavens and its eyes looked to the sunrise.

I was disgusted by the students who used to hide between rows of cotton to read books. "Either read or go pick cotton," I muttered to myself. I hid their books whenever I could. If only I were the chairman! I'd beat them about the knees with my stick and rip those books away! What good is reading? When you know that all the books have been censored and re-censored many times over, and there is nothing in them except words to steal your time. When you know that so many works of Lenin's have already been burnt, and that these, too, will soon outlive their expiration dates and disappear. When you know that everything you read will be wiped from your memory tomorrow. What good was reading, when you know that it doesn't quell the pain?

I wonder what needs to be done to take these city kids, who have no idea how important cotton is, or how to pick it, and teach them cotton farming. How do I make the kolkhoz chairman understand that these ridiculous students aren't helping with the harvest, and worse than that, they're hurting it? I don't know what the point is of bringing them here with their empty heads. Some can't get their noses out of their books, others can't quit their cigarettes and alcohol, and others spend all their time making out in the bushes.

Seeing all that made me furious. I felt bad for the land, the cotton harvest, and even the university. Why should it have to stand there alone and empty during the school year, without students, while they—foreign as they are to the land and the cotton—are made to go loaf around the fields? I just could not understand it.

As required, at eight o'clock in the morning, I exited the dormitory with my big folding cot, a suitcase full of clothes, and something to eat, and I marched toward the central university building. Lines of city buses were parked outside the main gates.

Today it was our turn, we students of the literature department, to head out to help our countrymen harvest cotton. Three or four other universities were supposed to go to the fields, too. All the buses in the city had been assigned to us students all week, and the only thing they would be doing for those seven days was shipping us out of the city and into the fields.

I remembered the birds that fly away to warmer climes when autumn comes. For us, it was the opposite: We had to abandon our cozy student nests and travel to meet the stinging winds of the steppe. Our motherland was summoning us.

The earth could hardly cope with the tracks we left, and it bore our marks on its skin for a long time after—from cigarette butts to tin cans and pornographic magazines, which the wind tossed from one end of the field to the other, and I kept worrying that, God forbid, some village boy would stumble across them and ruin his childhood. I felt sorry for the earth's whole being. How much effort would it have to expend to digest all these tin cans?

It had only been a week since I arrived in the city. Now here I was going back to the steppe. I still didn't know what corner of the country they were taking us to, where we would be staying, or what kolkhoz needed our help. We had to wait until the end of that first day to learn which district of this endless desert we would occupy for three months of our student lives.

A dozen police cars escorted us, showing the buses the way, to make sure they wouldn't get lost and would deliver the students to the field safe and sound. They set us up in a primary school which had closed its doors a week previously. All that school's students were out picking cotton.

There was a sign on one door: GRADE 5. We first-year students would be staying in this classroom. I unfolded my cot and lay down in the second row, facing the window. They put twenty-five of us in that room.

I looked at the walls and the door. They had been recently painted. Everything was ready for the school year. Probably the students had come to paint during their vacation. We used to paint our classrooms ourselves, too, and each of us painted our own desk and chair. But then, university students arrived from the city and took over the school for two months, and after they left, the school was much different from the last time we had seen it. The walls were full of nails and love notes and even obscene words that, if you happened to catch sight of one, would make you blush all over. And gum was stuck everywhere, even on the ceiling.

When you see people behaving like that, you feel as though an enemy has come to kick you out and occupy your personal territory. But for some reason, you still want to watch them eat and sleep, these tall, smartly dressed, good-looking young people, who for all we knew might be nice enough.

When it got dark, our innocent eyes flashed outside the school as we peeked curiously through the windows. And there was always a guard who would show up and whack our legs with a stick, but then a few minutes later we'd be back, peering into the classrooms again. The next day, it was sheer pleasure to tell our friends what we had seen the night before, asking each other, "Did you see that? Did you hear what that one said?" We gave all the students nicknames and sometimes we fell in love with them, or got mad at one of them for no reason, or started to hate them. One glance decided it all: good, bad, ugly, handsome.

There is a banging noise, like somebody is hammering something. I see that one of my classmates, a tall girl whose name I don't even know yet, is hammering a nail into the wall. "Hey! This isn't your house! You can't just make holes wherever you want."

I can feel ten or twelve pairs of eyes turning to stare at me at once, and then, as if in protest, in solidarity, without uttering a word, they all start hammering nails into the walls. Later I learned that a lot of the kids brought nails with them just for that purpose, on the advice of more experienced, older relatives. But I was the first person in my family who had gone off to the city and gotten admitted to the university.

The next day, when we returned from the fields, quite the sight greeted us: All the nails that had been put in the day before were torn out of the walls, and the clothes that had been hanging on them were tossed all over the floor. I broke out laughing, just bursting with joy that someone had taken revenge, on my behalf, on these spoiled city brats. But I also wondered who could have done it.

I looked automatically toward the window. It was dark. Impenetrably dark. I remembered what Mama had said: "Nothing goes unnoticed. There are always eyes that see how you behave."

It's now been eight days that I've been stumbling around this hospital, from all these segmentary notes to the videotapes and back again, and I still don't know why I lost my memory or why I recovered it again. Because I can't find Natasha. Because now that I've returned, Natasha—who came almost every day for those seven months and sat with me in this cramped, dark cell of a room and devoted so much energy to helping me bring everything back—is nowhere to be found. Where is she?

I take out the tape. What on earth had happened to make me run away on that last day of filming? I remembered what Mama had said: "It doesn't matter. Be happy you've gotten yourself together again, and you're back being the mistress of your own life. Fantasies are nice, but they aren't real life."

Snow is falling outside the window. Soft and monotonous. I climbed the stairs to the phone and called Natasha. "Natasha? Could you come this evening? I want to talk. I can't write. I'm so anxious. I can't write it down. I need to talk about it." I hung up and went back and sat on my bed. The wheel of my memory spun faster and faster. It was such a shame, such a shame that Natasha would miss these fragments… By the time she comes, I might forget. My thoughts seem to be sprinting, the same way I sprinted across the field.

I felt I was merging with the field, becoming one with it, because here I was like a fish in the water, confident in the sensation that I needed nothing and had no flaws. Because of all those classmates and teachers who got their backs up at my obtuseness, my refusal to learn my lessons, and who complained about me at this meeting and that meeting. Because the field gave me the ability to settle my scores with them all.

The established norm for students was thirty kilograms of cotton per day. I picked a hundred or a hundred twenty, and in only half a day. The rest of my time I spent lazing blissfully by the stream.

Those long hours of relaxation made me think about the profound essence of what was happening to me, about my existence as a human being in this world.

I always compared myself to cotton. The seed from which I developed seemed to resemble the cotton seed in that it was obliged to grow where it fell to the earth. It would ripen there and wither there. All my love and devotion to cotton aside, I suddenly felt that I wasn't like it at all. I was not a tuft of cotton, not the type to sit and wait for whatever hand would pick me this year. The gentle hand of a peasant woman, or the cold hand of a student, who would curse me as he harvested me. Or a tractor, which would roll full throttle over all my brethren in turn and churn up anything and everything in its iron talons.

I reach for a cotton bud, crooking four fingers as if I'm about to pick an apple from a tree. I feel the white cotton compressing under my touch, so softly, and springing back into shape again. It's like touching a breast, soft and gentle. I look around me. Students bend over and stand up, and by the way they move I can tell that they're smacking the cotton in the head and face, without love, without care, and yanking it out of the shelter of its little boll with no sympathy at all, and tossing it into the sacks knotted around their necks. Two bolls out of four are always left behind when they move on.

The steppe rings with voices from distant cotton plants. A lone remaining tuft of cotton has a weak, trembling voice. This cold autumn day, I look at the field. I am of the same blood as this field and this cotton. My soul is much more tightly tied to the two of them than to the tired, hungry students, torn from their homes, most of whom are outside the city for the first time, far from their mothers for the first time, all to harvest something called "cotton" from this field and then return to their studies and the lives they're used to. The pretty girls' hands, red and trembling from the cold, raise less pity in me than the unharvested cotton. If only I could separate those two contradictory things and never under any circumstances see those two enemies confront each other again—the cotton, and the students.

The snow fell, light and soft, from the sky. A few flakes settled on my eyelashes. I was glad it wasn't raining. Harvesting in the rain was impossible. Cotton touched by the rain becomes many times heavier, the earth becomes muddy, and walking becomes much harder. But from far off I hear the unhappy exclamations: "Hey now! Why snow? We want rain! Hey, you up there, God! Are you there? Are you listening?"

I smiled, almost invisibly. That was the same smile that appeared on my lips in the evenings, when the students would sit around the fire, sing, and recite their freshly written poetry. Even now I don't know what that smile means. Is it a smirk, or consent, or sympathy?

If it weren't for cotton, I think nothing else would have the power to occupy people all year round. It gives us work from early summer till late winter. From ploughing to seeding, from weeding to gathering the harvest; and then we use it to make winter feed for the livestock, and we collect the dry stalks for kindling to keep us safe from the cold. That work continues all year long. It is work with no end. The axle of human life.

There was a guy I was always avoiding who seemed to be the only one of my classmates who didn't avoid me, and once in a while, here and there, he even understood me. I don't remember his name. This boy was not the most capable student, and probably my indisposition toward our classes and to the university in general was where he sensed a kinship between us. That day he was holding a newspaper. He walked over to me as I sat by the fire and took the first seat available. A few photographs had caught his attention. I was curious about them, too. The pictures showed a newborn lamb with two heads, barely standing up. In Qaraqalpaqstan, on the banks of the Aral Sea, there were a lot of babies and lambs being born with two heads or six legs.

That was the first time I ever heard about the Aral Sea.

The director's voice rang out. "Stop!" He clapped his hands the way he usually did to get the attention of cast and crew.

Could a sea really dry up? I didn't believe it, in just the same way I had never believed that drops of water, drip by drip, could make an ocean.

"Well?" I ask.

He responds with a joke. "You've got miles and miles to go before you look like your mother. But it's much better than before, much better!" He put both hands on my shoulders. That must have been the first time he touched me. I could feel the warmth of those hands on my skin for a long time afterwards. It burned, like he had laid a hot iron across my shoulders.

He dismissed the crew and led me toward the tents. He held his hands under the faucet and let the water run over them, playing with it. His eyes looked happy and light. "I always wondered: what connects the water to the earth? But today I think I've figured out something important."

"What did you figure out?" I asked.

He tossed me a look then, and I still don't know what it meant. Maybe he wanted to ask me when I'd finally stop using the formal "you" with him, as he'd asked, or maybe he meant that if anyone should know, it would be me. But he answered a different way. "Together, they create, and without each other, they destroy."

I don't know what Mikhail was thinking about. That the shooting would come to an end, and he'd ride away on the train? Or that he'd leave and return to the editing table, to watch it all again? He told me, "Looking at you with the camera's eye is pure pleasure." He used the word "pleasure" so often that every time I stood in a shot I thought about that, about his pleasure. I felt as if the camera were covering for me, giving me the opportunity to look him in the eye, laugh, be bold and audacious. I could climb onto the tractor or stroll importantly through the white field full of cotton. And when I did, I could hold my head so high that I wouldn't even notice how the gentle steppe breeze ruffled my hair, tossing it side to side. I'd just go on gazing proudly at the sunset.

I let the heavy, oiled key to the tractor hang over my shoulder and I sang, louder and louder. My song blended with the roar of the tractor's motor and disappeared in the expanses of the field, dotted with people.

"How was my acting today?"

He squinted a little, pursing his lips a bit, and said, "Not too bad."

I jumped up and ran toward home. He never said a single nice thing about my work. He never let on that I was becoming a better actor every minute. He said it to other people, though.

I knew that he was preoccupied with the role of Mama, and I was preoccupied with his opinion. Or maybe with him, himself. During shooting, all our quarrels and squabbling made it clear to everyone, like it or not, that there was something between us. Mutual sympathy or mutual torture, I don't know, but whatever it was, it wasn't happening among the rest of them. Many times we filmed a scene exactly as he wanted, but he still had us do another take, five or six or seven more takes. Many times he said, "That's it for today. Enough! I can't get anything else out of this girl today," and the next day, he'd announce, "All right, next scene."

Maybe he was doing it all to help me get a better feeling for the scene with the kolkhoz chairman.

The kolkhoz chairman took my hands, opened them palms up, and proclaimed, "These hands do the work of ten men. Thanks to these hands, our country can hold its head high. These are the hands of a woman hero. And what a hero you are!" I look at my black, dried-out hands. Calluses on my fingertips, cracked from constant contact with cotton bolls. I jerk my hands back. My neck is as stretched out as ever, and my eyes are crowded with sparks of excitement. This kind of thing does not happen often.

Overflowing with pride, my eyes roam, looking for someone familiar, a friend or comrade, hoping the news would reach other people. The news that someone appreciates me. Finally, I've been noticed, among all these showoffs and freeloaders from the city! I let myself strut like a peacock. The sun was now barely peeking out from behind the hills, blinding my eyes. The bastard had finally done something nice for us! I was grateful to him, in the depths of my soul. Though I never would forgive him for stealing my freshness and youth, for making me an antisocial person, abashed by my own burnt skin and the web of wrinkles around my eyes and down my neck. I still haven't forgotten my younger face and beautiful white hands, and when I run into somebody, I burn with shame. I burn from sadness because—listen, everyone!—I, too, was beautiful once... Very briefly, and very long ago.

The chairman finished his speech and everyone stared at me. I had no idea what had just happened. The chairman gestured, as if to tell me to go ahead and say something, go on, dammit, why so mum? Squirming in embarrassment, I said, "Welcome, dear guests!"—and I smiled like an idiot, waiting for applause. Nobody applauded, except the chairman. Then he clapped me on the back with one of his heavy paws and escorted me from the stage.

They cranked up the music and the students started dancing. The chairman used one hand to encourage them to enjoy themselves and the other to hold me tight, just above the elbow, and steer me away from the crowd, a little faster than necessary.

I kept my head down as I walked, staring at the girls' short, colorful skirts. For a moment, I wondered how they could dance in heels like that. Mama's new galoshes and my brother's old pants were the nicest things I could find to wear to this party. I felt like my presence here was embarrassing the chairman. To be honest, I was embarrassed, too.

In my own district, even at the school I attended for ten years, I always felt like an outsider. I felt like an outsider in my own skin. That feeling has lasted for years now. When I look in a mirror or into somebody else's eyes, I understand it: I am not the woman I'd like to be. I know that the only place I feel at home is in the field.

We walked by the classroom where I sat at a desk for ten years, yearning for the lesson to end soon so I could go home, eat some bread, drink some tea, and head out to the cotton field. All those ten years in school left only one picture in my memory: the window. For ten years, different teachers came, said things, and left. On and on, until that longed-for May 25. Then, after ten years in school, I also left school. I mean that I graduated. I didn't run away. I put up with it until those ten years were over.

I've always loved this month of the year. When the students came to help, they dismissed us from class and handed over the classrooms to the young people. The school transformed into a dormitory. Now they had come to help again, so that we could finish the cotton harvest as quickly as possible, before winter set in.

I'm the deputy chairman of the collective farm now, so I know that the sooner the students come and go, the better. That means that the kolkhoz will have met its yearly quota and with the rest we can...we can... I have orders not to tell a soul.

I think the first thing I saw of the world outside was the field. Mama must have lifted me up, a newborn, as best she could, and held me to the window: "Look! Look, there it is, white gold! Our national treasure."

The cotton crop started outside our windows and extended as far into the distance as the human eye could see. But to tell the truth, those distances your eye is incapable of seeing in fact hold no cotton fields.

Mama says I was born in the cotton field, and they put her and me right on that tractor, the one I drive now, to bring us home. I asked, "Why didn't you go to the hospital?" She said, "People go to the hospital when they're sick. I wasn't sick, I was happy."

I take a look at the window frame. This frame, my fate, the borders of the cotton field: they are the same.

Natasha walked into the room holding a pack of paper. It had been almost a week. Natasha brought good news: There was a sixty percent chance my memory would return, and maybe, one of these days, I'd wake up as if from a coma and remember everything, and I'd be able to go home all by myself.

I put my pen at the start of a lined page in the notebook and thought for a bit. It's so hard to think. And it's hard to write when you don't remember anything, and what you do remember is not yours. People tell you, "This is yours, and that is not!" But you can't tell the difference, when the only thing that moves you is your headache and nausea. I wrote: *For two days now, the dizziness has been getting better and I haven't thrown up in bed once.*

Natasha came in, closed the door, and said, "I'm happy that you feel better and there's less pain." I wrote: *Smile. Happy. Bibi.*

I don't know if it was my mother or my grandmother, Mama or Bibi, who said, "A happy person is someone who travels the world and, in the end, is buried in the same patch of earth where his story began." We buried all our dogs in the garden, and I was wary of eating the fruit and vegetables that grew there. Now, I look at this endless cotton field and wonder: In which of its corners will I be laid to rest? It's a frightening thought. I turn off the tractor's motor. I think about the bone I once pulled out from under the wheels.

There is nobody around. Nobody dares come wander around this part of the field at this time of day. The earth exudes a fear that only I can live with. Mama says that my demons have been conspiring with the demons of the steppe. My concept of the world differs from that of people who were born in a warm bed, in a room with a ceiling. I'm afraid of houses and ceilings. There's a greater danger the ceiling will cave in than that the sky will fall. I have different work to do in the different seasons of the year. But my land and my tractor are always the same.

During my first days as a university student, I realized how heavy my gaze was. The light had left my eyes to travel far away. Sometimes toward the guy sitting next to me.

The voice of the instructor on duty rang out, urging us students back to the village school where we spent our nights. The snow on the bushes was the same color as the cotton. The skin on our hands had dried in the cold, and when I tried to lift my full sack of cotton off the ground, my skin literally cracked, and bloody crevasses appeared on the backs of my hands. I lifted my hands to my mouth, meaning to ease the pain with my warm breath. As soon as my lower lip moved, pain shot through it, as if it had been split in half. All I could do was tie the ends of my cloth bag to my wrists, which seemed to have more strength left in them. I couldn't lift the cotton I had harvested. I divided it into two bundles and dragged them by turns, two feet at a time, to the scales. Nobody came to my assistance. Their eyes told me plainly, "That's what you get for showing off. Enjoy your big haul."

Early each morning, the students decided how many kilos of cotton they would pick that day, depending on how the yield looked in each sector of the field. I was never satisfied with the agreed-upon quota and picked as much as I was used to picking with Mama and the local women. As much as the land had prepared for us. I felt as if I was the same breed as the cotton, and knowing that, my classmates looked at me and the field the same way.

That cold made me feel even more alone. When loneliness sets in, I think about warmth, body heat, and making love, like I've seen in the movies. The cold, humid steppe wind always reminds me of those things. Ever since I started working with the land, or in other words, as long as I've been aware of myself, I've seen the sensuousness that is in our people and noticed that the closer they are to the land, the more passionate they are. I don't know if it's the land or the sky that ignites this feeling in a person. Or is it that the gap between the land and the sky inspires fear, and pushes people to take shelter in each other's arms?

It was noon. I left the tractor windows open and climbed down, step after step, drowsy from the heat. A trembling danced across my body, and inside me I felt an unfamiliar, barely perceptible ripple of warmth. That pleasant ripple seemed to be tuning all the strings in my body, turning them tight. I felt as if I could sing and dance like I'd seen in ballet shows. But I wanted something bigger than singing and dancing. The heat was awakening a feeling in me that I could not name. I had never felt it before. The heat chased me toward the cool of the land, and as soon as I touched the soil, I felt lighter—no, I could feel myself sprouting. The sensation of growth, propagation... And I let the grasshoppers and ants, dying of thirst, crawl over my skin, so they could discover me, and I could discover myself.

Five o'clock in the morning. The shift nurse knocked at the door to my hospital room, and without waiting for an answer, walked inside. She carried a cup of coffee. She put the cup on the table and sat down on the corner of my bed. "Don't trouble yourself so much over the past, my dear, over what, thank God, is behind you. I don't know how much your search for Natasha will help you. But I'm worried that this will all have another unhappy ending."

I sat up in bed and took her hand. "You know where she is, don't you? For the sake of everything good you've ever done in the world, please, help me one more time. I can't do it. I need to find her. I need to know. Where did she go? I'm begging you." I squeezed her hand in both of mine, as if I were afraid she would run away.

With her free hand, she took the cup of coffee from the table and handed it to me. "It's getting cold. Drink up."

Her hand slipped out of my grasp. She stood up and walked to the door. "All right. I'll see what I can do."

I lay back down and lifted the cup to my lips, hands trembling. This fervor to uncover the past was overwhelming me. I reached for the old notebook, the one Natasha sent me. I don't know how many times I've lost myself in it already, while time and space cease to exist. In my mind, there were faces, becoming clearer day by day, spinning through the sky—sometimes cloudy, sometimes sunny. Sometimes those faces disappeared into one another. Natasha with Mikhail. Mikhail with my mother. Mama with me. Sometimes they merged together as if they were made of raw dough, and set themselves free again.

The play of colors in the lamplight was making my head spin. Natasha put something on the table she had cooked herself, and the tempting aroma rising from it took over my brain. I was unable to think of anything else. We sat at the table and centered between us the sweet pie Natasha had made in honor of the New Year. All we needed to go with it was some strong tea. Natasha pushed the call button near my bed and asked for tea. There was a gold watch on her wrist, and when she sliced the pie, it looked as if a magical serpent was wrapped around her crystalline wrist, its eyes shooting sparks.

Natasha asked, "Have you remembered anything?" That made me angry. She was always insisting that I remember something! What I have is enough for me. Natasha had barely entered the room when her eyes fell on my pillowcase, but she didn't say a word. I know she'll mention the writing there in a moment. But what I wrote is what I wrote, and that's it. It doesn't matter if it's reality, or whose reality. A person writes to breathe more freely. So the boulder crushing her chest slips off, so she can sense that lightness, and feel she's expelled all the poison from her mind.

But Natasha demanded to know what I was writing and why. As she took a bite of pie, her left hand traced over the pillow, trying to make out the words. How could anyone read that? I had tried to—and failed. It's as if something inside me wakes up while I sleep and forces my hands to write. So I write, quickly, without thinking about it. I write in order to make a record.

Goodbye,
Egotistical cotton,
Whose seeds—
Every one of them—
Took an ocean
To pour out its soul!

The young man who styled himself a poet wrote that with a ballpoint pen on the cloth sack he used to pick cotton. He and I always ended up at the scales together, one right behind the other. His bundle always weighed less than mine. Every time, there were more inscriptions on his bag. I was terribly curious to read them.

He wouldn't let me. Sometimes, I traded him a couple kilos of cotton for the right to read a few sentences. I liked to read that particular inscription of his over and over again. One evening, when we were sitting around a campfire, he sat down next to me. Suddenly he wanted to know why I liked those lines the best of everything he had written.

The expression "egotistical cotton" had occupied my mind so thoroughly that it seemed to have gotten into my blood and was now coursing through my veins. I say, "What do you mean by that?" He answers, "Nothing special. I wrote it after I saw a picture of the Aral Sea." The first time I ever heard of a connection between the sea and our cotton crop, I heard it from him.

A gentle rain was sprinkling down, and all the students were leaving the field, joking and fooling around. I touched a wet cotton boll and remembered what the young poet said.

This cotton you behold
Is a fish in the Aral's waters.

The gaze of a steppe wolf differs from that of a mountain wolf. In the steppe, keen vision and fast legs are held in the greatest esteem, but in the mountains what's important is the ability to jump high, from rock to rock.

They say I was supposed to be a tractor driver. But later they were worried a girl wouldn't be strong enough.

Ivan explained how it worked. "Look, there's the gas, there's the brake, there's the lever, there's the knob to release the poison to keep the worms away, this is where you switch over the rake, this is for tilling..."

The chairman issued an order. "Jump on up there. Let's see if you're any good for this work!" But I didn't remember a thing about what to press or why.

But I did remember being taught. It hadn't been the chairman who did it. And I pressed all the buttons in turn, amazed that this giant mountain of metal could be stirred with just a touch of my finger. I could make it go, and comb the earth's hair with it. I laughed in my amazement. I laughed! It was excited laughter, full of fear.

I unfolded my handkerchief and wiped the sweat off my neck and forehead. Ten years have passed since that day I so burned to become a tractor driver, and in every one of those years, I gained three or four kilos. Sometimes I think that by the time I made it to the tractor, nothing remained of my femininity and grace. Maybe they were never going to give me the tractor until I made myself more manlike? I learned life from the land, and I learned my way of life from the red kolkhoz tractor, which works the land with its love, frenzied and all alone. Its love affair with the land plays out differently at different times of year, but it never abandons it.

When it broke down for good, and its body tumbled to pieces, it dedicated itself to the earth's embrace and nestled down inside it. The last time I drove out to visit the kolkhoz lands, which no longer belonged to the kolkhoz, I saw that the only part of the tractor remaining was its big rake, fallen somewhere at the edge of the steppe, just like a dinosaur skeleton. The local kids were playing on it, jumping off and crawling between its steel ribs.

I told my father, "The tractor ought to be lying under this land." He looked at me with his good-natured smile. "All its components, right down to the smallest parts, have been snatched up and sold."

I looked out the window. Not a trace of the cotton field. They were building houses everywhere. Everywhere the endless cotton field had once been, from the upper canal to the lower canal, was built up with houses. As if since the time I left the village, everyone here had been doing nothing but building without interruption, day and night.

"Aftab! Take a step forward." On the last day of our labor practicum, the head rector of the university decided to start our meeting with an awards ceremony. He called me and four other people, and when we stepped forward, he shook our hands, thanked us, and gave us each a notebook. That was all we got for three months of work in the cotton field.

Years later, when I went to the Aral Sea, all I could see were the huge ships, sunk in the sand, with the ground-up bones of fish and birds. Just like the tractor in the earth. I wondered why it had never entered my mind to become a ship's captain and sail from one shore to the next. Maybe because aside from the land, I hadn't seen anything, didn't know or understand a thing.

But since I was little, I've been having a nightmare that repeats itself all summer. A ship bigger than the Titanic, docked in the earth behind the school, its horn letting out its last blasts before it embarks. Everyone is waiting for me. But I'm looking for something, as always, and the ship sets sail without me into the cotton field and floats away out of sight. It's always something small, a bathing suit or a suitcase or Mama's diary. But every time, I miss the boat. It's a huge white ship, its horn sounding sadly for thousands upon thousands of kilometers, so that I can hear it and perhaps catch up. But I'm right here, right here behind this window, just a second, wait just a second, please, I need to find Mama's diary! The diary? No, my swimsuit. Oh! Where's my suitcase? I'm drowning in sweat, my arms and legs thrashing under the covers. It left, it left, the ship is gone! I wake up sobbing. I was the loneliest, quietest girl in the district. Often I wouldn't even tell anyone about my dreams. Maybe nobody would have understood. Other people didn't seem to have nightmares, and I was afraid they'd laugh at me. A ship in a field? No, I couldn't tell anyone about those dreams.

When I stood in the Aral Sea basin and the wind tossed fine sand in my eyes, I realized why my classmates hated me.

That fall, when the Soviet Union fell apart, my heroism came to an end as well. I don't remember exactly whether my youth ended, and then the USSR, or if it was the other way around. But I do know that those two things are connected. Now I'm left here between two truths: the truth of the land, and the truth of the sea.

I sat under a tree with no leaves next to the road, spread out the cloth sack the young poet had written on, and let my eyes soak up his lines.

Before golden cotton
There was the golden fish of fairy tales.
Consider no kiss permissible
While the land mourns its split
From the water.

When the midwife took me by the hand and we went walking in the field, she used to tell me about the gardens of Samarqand. What I liked about those stories were the names. Crow Garden. Garden of Gold. North Garden. Paradise Garden. Upper Garden. There were more, too—I don't remember them all. The midwife told me that when you leave the village and walk into the city, you pass many, many gardens on the way.

I heard the crunch of something breaking under the tractor's wheels. By then, I was used to it, so I wasn't afraid. I left the stones to their fate. The truth was like a burial site, like a village cemetery, in that the newer and fresher it was, the more terrible it was; the older and more decrepit, the easier it was to destroy and forget.

My grandmother used to say that when she was young, every family used to plant as much cotton as they needed. But now, they plant cotton everywhere there is land, and people aren't allowed to harvest even one sackful or even buy it for money. "Your Bibi used to knit the most tiny, complicated things," she told me. "I dyed and dried a clump of cotton, spooled it around my toes, divided it into threads and knitted it. From collecting seeds to embroidery knots, I did it all myself, and I was so proud when I caught sight of my work on all the brides and grooms! Now, to buy yarn, I have to sit and wait for the gypsy merchants. But that string they sell has no tribe and no heritage, and nothing I make turns out any good."

The first time, I felt a lump rising in my throat, and I felt like screaming. Underfoot were shards of a ship, and a life saver.

A man on a camel was crossing the sea. The earth's skin was covered in cracks, and the camel's hooves got caught in them, and the animal rocked from side to side.

November 4, 1998.

Natasha came back from the movie theater. She had gone to see *White Gold.* She said they cut lots of scenes; it must have been the censor. He had done his job on it. I say, "I changed my mind. I want to see the movie."

"When?"

"Right now."

"You can't wait until tomorrow?"

"Tomorrow I might change my mind again."

Natasha laughed. "Well, then let's go."

The desert. Sad music. The camera begins to move slowly. A ship sunk in the sand. A young woman's white skirt, billowing in the wind. The camera pans to her skirt. It moves closer and disappears in the waving whiteness. It surfaces from those waves in a field of blooming cotton. The music intensifies, then is interrupted. On the screen, I see a woman putting her foot on the step of a tractor. She holds a red flag. The field is full of men and women, old and young. The woman has a wild look about her. Her proud eyes stare intently into the camera.

Natasha's eyes flash in the darkness. The music cuts off, replaced by the hum of people sitting off to the side or standing in line for food, tin plates in their hands. I don't remember the plot. The whole time I'm watching the film, I am thinking about why I still haven't moved into one of those ships that are drowning in the sand. Why have I stayed in that dark hospital room? What am I waiting for?

Everyone has left the theater. Only Natasha and I remain in our seats, our cheeks wet. I was weeping over the impenetrable darkness inside the ship. It was sad. The most hopeless thought was that after all that hard work, all that dreaming, we find ourselves in a lost corner of the desert, on a ship that no longer has the power even to blow its horn, to call you to say, "Let's set sail, let's cross to the other side! Let's sail the sea!" It was sad to think about the swimsuit I no longer needed. I didn't even need a suitcase anymore. The ship was nailed fast to a godforsaken desert.

Natasha looked at the desert and the ship, thoroughly dried under the baking sun, and the credits ran across them. That might as well have been the ship's burial. Natasha's arm was heavy across my shoulders.

A middle-aged woman with a mop waved at us to get out. I didn't feel like leaving the theater, or worse, walking away from the film.

Natasha took my arm. "Let's go." I held tighter to the armrests on my seat. I didn't want to go. We could watch it again! Ten more times, or even more, just watch and watch. Where is that girl, who must be all grown up now, and why did she put her medals at the feet of those rotting ships?

The girl who ran and ran, as fast as she could, running her heart out, while I sat there with my own heart beating so hard I could hear it booming all around me. And the narrator's voice, completely calm, intoning, "This is my older sister, running to help my mother…" My ears have gone deaf under the sound of my own voice, and I feel as if I can no longer hear anything but the sound of silence.

When I opened my eyes, there was a man with a gray mustache sitting by my bed, looking at me anxiously. I felt I had met that man somewhere before, and this wasn't my first time seeing that look.

He took my hands in his and buried his face in them. My hands grew wet, and the fact that I couldn't remember made me want to bang my head on the walls and the door. I wanted to yell at the top of my voice, but I stared quietly at this middle-aged man's gray hair. He lifted his head and looked me in the eye. "It's me. Mikhail. I can't believe you don't remember me." The nurse hurried in, led him out of the room, and closed the door soundlessly behind her.

Natasha appeared, looking frightened, a tense smile on her face. She walked over to the chair and sat down. That's where the man had been sitting. Just like he had done, she took my hands and brought them to her lips. Her eyes were red as if she hadn't slept. I squeezed Natasha's hands tightly and wanted to never let them go.

No date.

I sense that Natasha, when she reads my notes, will again say nothing for a long time. I sense that my notes no longer make her happy. I sense that she is tired of me, and worst of all, I seem hopeless to her now.

The Young Poet arrived from Samarqand, and every day, he taps a light drumbeat on my door and comes in. He brings flowers. Natasha said that the Young Poet is my husband. But he himself has said nothing about that. He reads a few poems, holds my hands to his heart, and says goodbye.

I feel more free with him because, with him, I feel no obligation. He asks nothing of me, never asks that I remember him. He seems glad that I've forgotten everything.

Yesterday, in one of his poems, he wrote,

The past is nothing special.
The future is nothing special.
Just a wild poppy, torn in the wind.
But today
A moment of freshness—
Your gaze
On my face.

The Young Poet gives me much more. He talks about things my heart longs to hear. And he never mentions people I don't know, or whom I'm supposed to remember. He talks about the present day and does not drag the past around with him.

My only option was to recognize people by the look in their eyes. And his eyes alone could give me peace or convey his worry. Everyone who considered themselves close to me seemed to carry a passport in the way they looked at me. When you don't recognize someone, the fear in you multiplies a thousandfold.

I looked at the young woman who was sitting next to me and trying hard to hold back her tears. There was something incomprehensible in those eyes. A meaning similar to the one behind my previous visitor's words, when he said, "I can't believe you don't remember me."

Mama appeared in the distance, walking with her head held high, her shoulders broad as ever. As she neared, I could make out the drops of sweat on her face. With every step, the medals pinned to her chest clanged like bells.

Natasha never took her eyes off me. Maybe she meant to record my every move in her diary. But I was calmly watching the moves of the woman who was my mother, the woman with so many medals.

That clanging of Mama's medals, in time with her steps, rang all night in my head. I just could not believe that woman was my mother.

Chewing a thin green leaf, Mikhail walked up and sat by the fire, facing me. Skipping any preliminaries, he said, "You know, I think you've made one mistake, and you're stuck inside it." I looked at him in surprise. It made me angry that in these last days of shooting, for some reason, everyone had gotten it into their heads to start lecturing me and giving me instructions. Everyone wanted to offer me friendly support, as if I were stuck in the mud. Someone said, "Yes, come on, put that foot here." Someone else said, "No, don't move, you'll get even more bogged down." Someone else: "Why did you even decide to tramp through the mud in the first place?" Someone else: "We've all been through this before, or we'll have to go through it later." I was angry. But I looked at him calmly. Let him talk, now, while the flames of the campfire leapt into the air and made my cheeks feel hot. He grinned in a way that meant he understood everything, yes, he knew what I was thinking, and he said, "You keep comparing your life with your mother's, weighing them against each other on the scale. You shouldn't do that. Each life has its own value. They're the different experiences of two different branches of history."

Thick tobacco smoke hung over the roadside café. An Asian-looking man came to the window and asked for a cigarette. The sound engineer held out his pack of cigarettes without opening it. The man took one and thanked him with a nod of the head. He lit it as he walked away, looking at us. I glanced at the sound engineer and asked, wordlessly, "Do we know him?" He shook his head no. The man slowly moved away. He reminded me of the kolkhoz chairman, except he was older and generally more tattered. Maybe it really was the chairman. But maybe not.

I stared at the cigarette smoke. All smoke is surprisingly similar. It rises from a point, and you can never see where it soars off to, where it disappears, but the wider it spreads its skirts, the greater the effect it creates. Mikhail made that comparison once when we were watching the fire one night. Mama was worried about how the film would turn out, and Mikhail tried to reassure her without making any promises. Then he picked up a piece of kindling and brought it close to a red flame. "We're at this step. This is the step when the ideas burn and the story is created. We don't know how far the smoke will rise, or where it will go."

I looked at the fire then and thought that he was right. Nobody on that steppe had ever set a campfire before, and it could be that nobody ever would again. The film crew brought light to the steppe of my life and Mama's, to the steppe planted with cotton, where darkness reigned at night, and the sun reigned during the day. I was more worried that the filming was almost over. What was I going to do when they took down the tents and got on the train? What was I going to do? Back to the university, or...? I couldn't remember if I had ever done anything before I began working on the movie. It was like a new chapter in a book, with no relationship to the previous one. When I was moving forward, the past constantly disintegrated, or more precisely, it lost all its value and meaning.

Long days watching the movie camera working and observing the process of setting it up had taught me to think about the future, to craft a new story, without getting stuck in the past, without lingering even in the scene we had just finished shooting. "When it's over, forget it. Move into the next scene in a new state, with a new attitude." Those words from Mikhail were a constant refrain ringing in my ears.

I was astounded by his fresh view of life, his dissimilarity to everyone else. Every time his feet trampled all over something else I held dear, he tortured me, but something told me not to resist, that he was right. Something pushed me to escape rotting in place, to open myself to things that were new to me—with difficulty, with tears, but also with a pleasing feeling of agitation.

Mikhail seemed to be the ship of Mama's nightmares. The ship that was blowing its horn, saying, "Come here, make sure you don't get left behind!" But I always found a reason to be late. A reason to be late for the ship sailing up to my doorstep, bearing signs from a new world. A reason to stay. Something deep in my soul always told me, "Stay. Defend your faded holy relics."

My cigarette has burned out, no smoke left inside it. I look at the sound engineer. He is also buried deep in himself, and his gaze seems to have traveled through the window and not returned. As if he understands that I now have a clearer picture of my seven months of illness, but no longer any need for words and conversations. As if there is no point in discussing it. The silence between us is more eloquent.

But I feel like asking one small question, asking him why... Why hadn't Natasha been involved in the filming from the very start? But why should I break such a beautiful, calming silence?

There was a storm in his eyes, one I recognized; it came with the whirlwind that sometimes fogged his pupils. But the silence! It was infectious as a disease, that silence.

The cigarette was forgotten between his lips. A thin stream of smoke stretched upward, alongside his femininely delicate nose. There was calm in his silence. If he had said, right then... If he had sat down next to me and said what was troubling him, then maybe none of this would be happening right now. Maybe my daydreams wouldn't have taken such deep root in the salty soil.

It was Natasha's mother who told me why she hadn't arrived earlier, with the rest of the crew. Natasha was trying to keep her distance from Peter, the sound engineer, whose feelings were a burden to her. Peter was crazy about Natasha, Natasha was crazy about Mikhail, and Mikhail was crazy about his work.

Natasha was the one who had handed Mikhail the newspaper and said, "Here's the subject of your next film." She wanted to gather up everything Mikhail could love, everything he had any interest in, and make him fall in love with her. She would buy his attention.

I look Peter's hand. "I'm going. I want to see her." He looked left, then right, as if searching for the quiet that had just been shattered.

The more I learned, the farther I was moving away. But I still wanted to learn more. I began to feel the hatred that shapes love. Or perhaps love, mixed with hatred, was awakening inside me.

Natasha's mother went to bring in the tea. She was gone for a while. I examined the walls again. The living room was frozen in the seventies, judging by the smell of the wallpaper. Dusty curtains spoke of the indifference the mistress of the house felt to whatever went on outside. A spiderweb was wound cozily around the television antenna. The only shiny thing here was the glasses arranged in a row in the wooden sideboard.

I got up and went into the kitchen. Natasha's mother stood motionless, staring at the tea kettle decorated with lilies. I glanced at her face, wanting to know what turmoil she was suffering in such deep silence.

From the doorway, I took another look at the walls. A photograph of Natasha, faded and slightly thinned from the heat and damp. Mikhail's arm was over her shoulders. They were both smiling as they looked at me.

I spent some time trying to imagine what they were smiling about. What moment of what day was recorded here?

The car stopped next to the canal and honked. The whole film crew started clapping their hands. "She's here! Natasha is here!" Only two people stood still, as if turned to stone: Peter and me. The entire crowd of people ran to the car. Slowly, a door opened. A woman stepped out, and immediately tucked herself away from the sun, under a white hat. She took a white scarf from around her neck and used it to wave hello to the crew. I felt that I needed to get out of there. That white greeting meant grim news for me.

Peter took my hand and led me toward the crowd. Dry clumps of earth melted softly under the soles of my shoes. Cotton-plant thorns left scratches on my knees. But my eyes were fixed on the hands of Mikhail and the girl in white. Mikhail took the visitor's hands in his, pressed his lips to her white skin, and gazed into her eyes. The kiss lasted an eternity and lit the fires of hell in my heart.

My hand slipped out of Peter's. A weight pressed on my shoulders. Without tearing my eyes from this silent scene, I walked off toward the tractor. A few steps and I was running. I ran to take shelter from all those eyes. I wanted a miracle to occur and wipe me out of all their memories in a flash. Jealousy—or, no, shame—flared hot, and its scorching fire devoured my entire life.

Natasha's mother looked from me to the photo. "You didn't know?"

"No."

I didn't ask what, I expressed no curiosity; I just repeated it: "No." She told the story easily, like a tale that was on the tip of everyone's tongue. My feigned indifference ensnared her, and she told me everything.

Mikhail and Natasha had known each other for many years. Their friendship grew as they began working on joint projects. If they hadn't gone to Central Asia, they might have moved in together. An article in who knows what newspaper changed everything.

Natasha's mother was beginning a story in which there was no place for me. I watched her lips move to guess which words she was saying. The noise of the tractor was getting louder, and it kept me from hearing, kept me from stepping outside that field, illuminated by the very presence of the girl in white. I could not tear myself away from the ring of people who seemed to want to shelter themselves from the sun under her wide-brimmed hat. They stood tightly crowded around her.

Natasha's mother was saying, "One day she read in a newspaper about how a woman was walking around the Aral Sea collecting fish skeletons. I think the headline was something like 'Mistress of the White Gold,' and it was about this woman from Central Asia. This woman had been named a Hero of Labor and worked for a long time as a kolkhoz chairman, but then, after the Soviet Union collapsed, she and her eight children were out of work; they were barely making ends meet.

"They both fell in love with that story, and they went to search for that woman—and they found her. But I don't know what happened there to make Natasha not go along with the film crew later. Maybe she was trying to avoid Peter."

The tractor's noise is still thundering in my ears. I was in both the past and the present simultaneously, and as I headed for the canal, I asked Natasha's mother, "Why?"

She couldn't help it: she burst out in tears. She wrinkled her red nose and said, "She was pregnant."

The tractor collided with the barrier to the canal. The earth swayed. Time shuddered and disappeared.

When I repeated, again, "Yes, I want to see her," Peter inhaled his cigarette smoke with an audible rush of air. This time, the voice did not belong to me, and it was not patient and gentle. This voice was tired, or perhaps resolutely sober, evidence that all patience had evaporated. Peter held the cigarette in his teeth, dug in his pocket, and pulled out a pen. He scrawled something onto the cigarette pack. Then he stuck that hand back in his pocket and took his cigarette into his fingers again. He laid his hand on mine. "Good luck to you. God protect you."

On his way out of the café, he made a fist, and thumped himself a few times over the heart. He used to do that frequently during filming, when he was excited or upset. His smile warmed up the whole café. On the package of cigarettes, Peter had written Natasha's address in Poland.

He had always slipped in quietly, unnoticed, and left abruptly. Peter was unpredictable. But here he had delivered, into my hand, the key to the treasure I had been searching for. There was only one thing I could do, and that was the thing he had thought so much about doing.

I put Natasha's address and Peter's cigarettes in my purse and raised a hand, asking for the check. A thin girl came to the table. Her smile glowed, but my face was dark and full of the unknown, like the address on that flimsy paper package.

Nina-hanum knocked on the door and came straight in. "Why didn't you come down to dinner? I told them to bring our plates here. We can eat together."

My head lay as immovable as a millstone on the pillow. I felt no connection between my head and my body. "You slept too much, so you have no appetite," said Nina-hanum. "But I won't allow you to stop eating. I'm not leaving you alone until you eat this all up."

Nina-hanum had tried many times to talk me out of traveling to Poland. Meanwhile, I was going out of my mind trying to send these feelings that had awakened within me back into my dreams and oblivion. I wanted to immerse myself in water to wash my mind clean of everything that was tormenting me. But what was that? I didn't know. Natasha's pregnancy, or the fact that Mikhail was the father of her child?

I felt terrible, and stupidly, I felt disgusted with myself. Who did I think I was, insinuating myself into other people's relationships and refusing to leave? No. I had to go, to see once and for all whether or not I had as much courage and kindness as Natasha. Could I hold a woman in love to my heart, tend to her, wish her well?

It seemed I had split in two and was arguing with myself. I said what Mikhail would have said if he were here. "What talent you have for weighing yourself on other people's scales! First your mother's, for so much time, and now you're comparing yourself to Natasha, wondering if you can do what she does! Why don't you appreciate yourself for what you are, sweet thing? Why always put yourself on somebody else's path through life?" But the other half of me said, "No! You must figure it all out, untie the knots, or you'll never have peace."

I was still holding the receiver in my hand when a woman rapped on the glass door of the phone booth. The tractor noise in my ears faded and died out. It was replaced by a voice over the loudspeaker announcing that boarding was about to close for the Moscow–Warsaw flight. The Moscow–Warsaw flight! I would have to hang up and race away. Natasha had a happy voice infused with light. "Oh my dear, my Mahtab, my Aftab!" It was a gentle, maternal voice, as if I were still sick and she were still my doctor, my helper, my protector, my support. "Thank God you're in Moscow! Thank God a thousand times that you called. I didn't know what to do, darling, I was about to burst... Mikhail and I wanted to go to Samarqand and see all of you, we missed you so much." Feeling nothing, I hung up and opened the door for the woman, who was clearly in a hurry. "Go ahead, I'm done talking."

When I landed at Chopin Airport in Warsaw, a light rain was falling. With every deep breath I took, a calmness grew inside me, and it spread through my whole body. Chopin had been playing throughout our flight, soft and silken, and the leaves dropped away, one by one, from the tree of my anxiety. As I listened to Chopin, I thought about his fingers moving. They were as fleet as those of a young woman picking cotton.

"50 Bronislaw Czech Street." The taxi driver repeated it twice.

"Yes..."

"We're here."

I looked around me again.

"Has it changed a lot?" The driver must have thought I had been here before, and now I was returning and not recognizing the place. I cut off that conversation at the roots by handing him the money. I had no clear reason in mind for being here. What had I come to do? Repeat a past mistake, or stir up a storm that had calmed?

I thought I might have come in order to walk Natasha and Mikhail's street, smoke a cigarette, and go home. Natasha's voice on the phone had cured all my yearning to see her. Instantly, my curiosity had vanished.

In front of the building, there was a middle-aged woman playing with some children. A man was staring out an open window, enjoying a breath of fresh air. The woman used her hand to shade her eyes from the sun and shouted, "Igor, come down!"

Life was seething green all around me, and I could smell water. Maybe Mikhail enjoyed a window like that one. Maybe his window opened onto the green lake and let him watch the small sun move. I walked around the edge of the front yard. With every step, my posture grew straighter.

The environment was different here. The sea was green and full to the brim, the steppe was diluted with the seeds of every enormous tree, and tall buildings set down their feet on the breast of the land. Here things were somehow different, and I could see differently, too. Live differently. Think differently.

What do Mama, Nina-hanum, and Natasha's mother think when they stand before a mirror? About the buildings that were built, the land that was developed, and the generations that they brought into the world? I had come to express my thanks, but now I realized I needed to ask forgiveness. I seemed to be acknowledging that I had plopped myself down, like a child, in the most tender moments of Mikhail and Natasha's life.

Natasha's mother had treated me like family, and when she spoke about the past, she never used my name. Maybe she didn't want to confuse the past and the present. Or maybe it was because of all the different names I called myself while I was ill, the names I immediately forgot. Or maybe she had simply hoped that I would find her daughter. I don't know why, but I started to feel close to her. And also profoundly guilty. Everyone was woven into life except me. I was stuck in the closed loop of the distant past. What am I doing, actually? What do I want?

Usually, when my thoughts take this turn, night has fallen outside my window and I have nothing else to do. The nights stretched long and straight, while the days were heavy and short. It was time to leave Moscow and go home to my mother. But my heart was still tied to this place, tied by something that had no name. Maybe the thread was a lie I had spun to put off my meeting with Natasha and Mikhail. A lie that lamented in my heart while my tongue would not move to speak it.

When I closed my eyes, I felt free, as if my legs were no longer fettered, as if I had been stumbling in a dark cave. I remembered the words, but I had forgotten how to pronounce them, forgotten their color and scent.

I wanted to write. But what? In what language? For whom? Mama had me, Mikhail had Natasha, Nina-hanum had all her friends and colleagues. And Peter visited Natasha's mother now and then, smoked a cigarette, and pined away before the photograph in the kitchen.

The sky looked gloomy, and a dark thundercloud was quickly lowering itself over the earth. Did the wind blow clouds, or did they move under their own power? I didn't know. Either way, it was terrifying. Not knowing was terrifying. I didn't know where that cloud had come from. East or west? Why did it even matter? I didn't know why east and west mattered. Which way was east? There was nobody around I could ask. The terror had me completely in its grip. I wanted to squeeze myself into a corner and draw a little sun there.

I felt the same way I had on the day Mama arrived from Samarqand and sat down next to my bed. Natasha had left then, soon to return, so we could all go to the movie theater again to see *White Gold*. When I was alone with Mama in that room, I knew which place in the world my soul, and mind, and body belonged. I knew where in this world I was lying, sick, and where I had come from, and where I was going.

We sat in the theater waiting for the show to begin. After a long silence, Mama brushed her fingers over the medals she wore on her chest. "Do you know what they gave me these for?" I shook my head, even though I wished she didn't expect any answers or questions from me.

Mama pointed to the first medal, which looked like a gold coin wrapped in red and green scraps of fabric. "Nineteen seventy-five, for achievements in protecting the natural resources of the state. I was pregnant then, carrying you under my heart, my eighth little one. And this medal they gave me for bearing my eighth child. The day that I got it, I wasn't the only one. There were a hundred women like me, lined up in a row, so their service could be recognized. Some carried pictures of their sons who had died in the war in Afghanistan."

Nothing Mama said moved me. I wished she would stop talking, wished she wouldn't utter a word. Her eyes and her nose were running, and she wiped them with a handkerchief. She lowered her head. "But I wasn't a bad mother. I did my best so you never got a glimpse up close of these worries. I never allowed even the toes on your feet to touch the land in the cotton field." She clutched a hand hard to her heart. I thought she must be in pain. I didn't feel well. No, for some reason I felt afraid of this woman. I looked around, searching for Natasha.

I wasn't listening to Mama anymore; all my attention was directed at the screen. That was my second time watching the film with Mama. *White Gold*. I loved the ending best of all. A girl with a red kerchief stands in the middle of the cotton field and watches the sun set. The wind ruffles her skirt. Mama said, "Those were the clothes you were wearing when they took you to the hospital. The director kissed your kerchief and gave it to me. I knew what he was about. I knew that he loved you. I gave him the kerchief to keep. I wanted him to make sure you were all right."

Thousands of men and women came together to dig enthusiastically in the earth, opening a path for the water so that it could return to the sea. Exactly how, several decades before, all the water that was flowing toward the Aral Sea was rechanneled to the plantations, to the lands where cotton grew. But now, it's too late. The Aral Sea has a broken heart, and in the face of everyone's indifference, it's taken its own life. Drop by drop, it turned its sweet waters to poison which it dispensed to everyone around it. Without love, even a sea has no power.

Mama wrote in her diary, *If I could, I would pour out the waters of the ocean toward Asia, toward the Aral, toward Zarafshan, into the scorched deserts of Samarqand and Bukhara.*

Fearful, I took her hand. It was easier here in the darkness of the theater. I was holding the hand of the woman who owned everything I could remember about my life. This woman might as well have come here to say that aside from her, I had nothing.

When we reached the cotton field, Mama started her story. "You must listen closely, and then tear my memories out of your head like weeds, and leave only your own growing there. This is the field where you recreated my life. You recreated it and fell right into it. You learned the film's story by heart, and you drowned yourself in that story."

Mama pointed to the bank of the canal. "This is where the camera spun for two whole months, and you played a role, all the time trying to please a man for whom nothing except the film seemed to have any importance. My little girl, crazy with love... That was love in you, a love I've never felt. I never was able to tie my heart to a single man like that." Mama looks at her old, wrinkled hands. "But not giving away your heart might be better than giving it to the wrong person. I don't know."

Mama told me about what went on behind the scenes in the film. That was the story I had written in confused fragments those past few months, wherever I could find the room. I wrote so as not to forget. Or maybe so I would forget. With every word Mama spoke, a curtain seemed to lift, and light returned to my eyes.

The field was full of people going about their usual business: picking cotton. Mama and I drew attention despite ourselves.

A man in a uniform came up to us. After introducing himself, he said, "I'll have to inspect your bag, sister."

I looked at him in surprise. "Why?"

He answered, "Foreigners are not allowed to enter this territory."

"I'm not a foreigner!"

Mama took a step back. Joy flashed in her eyes. She had recognized my voice—my own, genuine voice. That was me, and I was defending myself with my own voice.

"I was born here. This is my native land!"

"I apologize, but I'll need to ask you to come with me to the car."

My pale skin, untouched by the sun, revealed that either I wasn't from around here, or that I'd stayed away from the all-seeing eye of the sun here for too long. For this policeman, those two possibilities had the same meaning. My gaze caught things I hadn't seen while we were shooting the movie. It was as if my trip to Moscow had lifted a yellow film from my eyes. I could see colors more clearly, and signs more precisely, and the policeman took note of the change immediately. He noticed the comparisons waving like a banner in my eyes.

"I apologize, but you'll have to go back immediately."

I try to pull my arm away from him. "I need to see my friends. I grew up on this land. My umbilical cord blood spilled on this land."

"That has nothing to do with me. Please don't waste everyone's time, hanum."

"What is this place I've come to, a prison? How can you treat people this way? Here's my passport, and here, look, this is the address where I live."

The man's tone became slightly less stern. "One quick meeting, then you go right back. No photographs. No long conversations."

Now hatred exploded within me, hatred for every kind of subjugation. Paying the man no attention, I walked to mama. "Mamajan! Mama!" We embrace and stand like that for a long time, breathing in each other's scent.

"Welcome home, my daughter. Welcome home!"

Now that I've found everyone, I want to forget them.

I sat down near the door, where I spent so much time from birth to age twenty-five, in the house from whose front doorstep I could hear the sky. But I never understood when it sang in my ear, "Watch out, watch out! They'll pluck off your head like a cotton boll here!"

I couldn't sleep. My face was turned to the dark hotel room window, and I couldn't take my eye off the sky over Warsaw. The telephone rang for the first time. I remembered with a start where I was from and why I was here. It was the front desk with a message from Nina-hanum. ""If she calls again, please tell her I'm not here, that I've stepped out. No, say 'She went back to Samarqand and she'll get in touch.'" I never did call her back. All I did was find a postcard with a view of old Samarqand, and write on it, *Thanks for showing me so much kindness. I'm back in my own life, my everyday routine. Forever yours, Mahtab. Samarqand.*

For a whole week, I walked around Warsaw. Just as Moscow is full of people, Warsaw is empty of them, and full of greenery.

I never tired of walking, and I never worried even a little that I might get lost. But I seemed to always be walking in circles around one little café with a view of the river, where I had a favorite table. Sometimes it poured, and I had to step inside. But on nice days, I sat outside and watched the river. I have never been a real fan of coffee, but the aroma of the freshly roasted beans dissolved the intoxicating cloud of Samarqand's tea in my mind. Often my undrunk coffee went cold, and my eyes happened to fall on a woman walking her dog past the café tables. She looked homeless. Her dog had disheveled, damp fur—it was even shabbier than its mistress, who walked past the café staring straight ahead. She walked slowly, the dog leading the way. Sometimes the dog would look back, as if it wanted to make sure the woman was still following.

On my last day, when I had already decided to leave, I set off to follow the woman with the dog. I couldn't resist my curiosity. Where did she go every day along this road?

The street led to a square. The dog stopped worrying about the woman falling behind and trotted faster, and when it reached the statue in the middle of the square, it sat down at its base. The woman sat down next to it, took something from her pocket, and lifted it to her mouth. Bread, probably, I thought. But suddenly, the mournful voice of a flute rang out. The dog turned to the statue and started to howl, singing along, and people gathered around them. I looked at the statue. A woman holding a sword, but naked. As I walked away from the square, I turned back and took another look at the crowd. But I saw something that made me walk back to the statue again. The woman with the sword had a tail, like a fish.

When I ran my hand over the mermaid's body, the sea gleamed in the folds between her scales. This was the water peri who, to thank the people for freeing her, turned herself to stone to protect their city.

Warsaw made my shoulders straighter. I cast the whole heavy load I had carried from Moscow into the waters of Warsaw. Now I was free of the past, and my heart was looking for the future—a future which still stood, as confused as ever, on the cobblestone streets of Samarqand.

But I couldn't leave without saying goodbye to the young man with the nice smile. Every time I came to the café, he gave a little bow and walked to the staff door in the back. I had sat in that café for hours, putting my thoughts in order, coaxing my memories out into the light, evaluating which ones I ought to keep.

The young man did not appear. I called over the waiter. "What do you have to eat?" When he brought my order, I asked, "What's the name of that young man who's here every day?" "Do you mean Lukasz?" I shrug. "If I knew, I wouldn't be asking." We both laugh. He says, "Lukasz is the owner's son. He'll probably stop by at his usual time." I say, "Today is my last day in Warsaw." I wanted to add that I didn't know why I wanted to say goodbye in person, but thought it probably didn't matter. Why did I want to see him, anyway? I didn't know.

When I had paid my bill and was about to leave, there was Lukasz at the door.

"Hello!" I said, joy in my voice, and a little more quietly, "And goodbye."

"Are you leaving?"

"Yes, this is my last day in Warsaw."

"You're not from here?"

"No."

"Where are you from, then?"

"Samarqand."

"Oh, Samarqand... How interesting." A man was waiting to come into the café, and we were in his way. I moved a few steps aside. Lukasz followed me. He took another step. So did I.

We kept on walking that way, asking each other silly questions. I think he was also only speaking half-truths. Sometimes I think that people's past and even their present are not important to me. What is important is their presence, right this minute. Their palpable presence, in which there is either a charming glance or some display of kindness—to make their behavior that much more authentic. Or, as Mama says, the stars come together in people, and even when they're not acquainted, they feel close to one another, they feel at ease. Lukasz's star was warm. It wasn't one of those glacial stars that hang between the earth and the sky and radiate a chill, even from a distance.

Suddenly, I felt how necessary these things are: unhurried strolls like this one, people I don't know, other people's life stories. As if my own story was a blossom that had withered and worn out. I no longer wanted to compare myself with other individuals. Instead, I posed my own life against the lives of multitudes of other men and women, from other countries, and my pain and memories became easy to bear. My own little stories and worries were forgotten. I asked him short questions about his recent and distant past. I wanted to listen, and as I did, the knots of my own memories unraveled, and truly disappeared. They gathered up their skirts and made way for Lukasz's new, fresh stories.

We walked slowly and spoke with each other warmly. It reminded me of the Russian movies where a couple meet on the street and the plot unrolls from there.

I opened the door. My hotel room was a royal mess, and my own laziness seemed to be seeping out of everything. It was all outside my power, or otherwise I would have asked Lukasz to wait in the hall while I gathered up the clothes strewn everywhere. But I didn't. I didn't want him to think I was hiding anything, or ashamed of anything. As if he were me. As if I were walking into this room with myself. As if Lukasz were the fruit of my imagination, and before him, nothing could stop me. As if I had known him for years, and he was sweet and dear to me. Now we said nothing as we unfastened our buttons, one at a time. Eye to eye. No words. No signs. As if this weren't the first time. There was a surprising self-confidence radiating from my skin. A fine desire, natural as wanting a drink of water, ran like a current between us.

Without touching hands, we sought each other out with our lips, and they came together and we drank and drank. More powerfully, more voluminously, every time.

That thirst rose up inside me, a very womanly wanting, and when a broken moan burst from my throat, I remembered everything. I remembered holding hands with Mikhail, coming a step closer, moving a step apart. The warmth of his body made our dance hot, sweat trickled down my cheeks, and he said, "You're so innocent." The clothing I had tossed on the bed fell to the floor, and we consumed each other, like the flames of a fire, exhaling only heat and smoke. It was as simple as that for the two of us to make love. No torment, no pain, no expectations. Lukasz's hands drank in my body, wandered all over it, lingering on my shoulders. I could see the sun in the curls of his hair. The last moan poured out of me. Traces of blood decorated our bodies in delicate patterns when we looked in the mirror, laughing. It was as simple as that for me to conquer my wild fear of masculinity, a fear that, for me, now carried no danger of violence, no threat of a broken heart. Naked, we spun before the mirror. Warsaw spun with us. As I dropped onto the bed, I remembered everything, and in my mind, I thanked my past, and forgave it. The hands of this young man I had only just met were the scales of a balance that weighed my whole life in a new way.

When I looked out the train window, my thoughts were far beyond the boundaries of Mama's diary, but in my head, everything was arranged as neatly as the shelves of her library. I remembered the color, size, and title of every book, and the other details didn't bother me. Mikhail was there, on a shelf in the archives of my memory, like a heavy, green volume. And like any other book I'd read, that one no longer excited me. Nina-hanum was a book, too, a book of folktales Mama read to me at bedtime, and I never wanted her to stop, so I could listen and listen forever... Natasha was probably a poetry collection. Full of lyrical verses, and when you recite one line, the whole poem comes to life in your memory; but if you forget a line, the rest is forgotten as well.

Mama herself was an ancient epic, maybe the *Shahnameh,* and I could see parts of her soul in every book I had ever loved. The *Shahnameh* was packed with fields of battle, fields of self-sacrifice.

Women with cotton stalks piled in their arms, their faces wrapped for protection from the sun, sent the good news to the passengers on our train. Who said that peris don't exist? Then who are these peris, half women, half buried in the land? My peris of the steppe! I know that if your legs were free of the land, if your arms were free of that cotton, you would rush to the sea. You would dive headfirst into the sea of your drowned dreams. You probably dream of ships, blowing their horns from dusk to dawn...

I speak to the old man sitting next to me, buried under memories of his youth. "Do you know why we never see mermaids or sea peris anymore?" He shakes his head. "Because they came long ago to hide in the steppe." The old man smiles and waves at the women in white, up to their waists in the field. That might be too little, so he blows them a kiss.

The old man is a schoolteacher. "You're not retired?" I ask him, surprised.

He says, "I was once. But everyone moved away. Hardly anyone stays for a tiny teacher's salary."

I still couldn't tear my eyes from the endless steppe. Near the railroad tracks, some schoolchildren were sitting around a samovar. Somebody waved. The boys threw pebbles at the train, a thing they might never have the chance to ride. There were girls washing dishes in a canal. Cotton was planted everywhere, across the whole space between the earth and the sky.

Since I hadn't finished my university degree, I couldn't hope for more than a job teaching first grade. I hated the university and every other contact I had with our obsolete system of education.

I walked into the room and gave the children an embarrassed look. "Salam. I'm your new teacher. My name is Mahtab." That was the first time I had ever pronounced my name with confidence. In one voice, the children shouted, "*Sal-am!*" I laughed, fully and genuinely. I remembered my own childhood. I wonder how long schoolchildren have been greeting their teacher in chorus, and how that came about. But what was wrong with it? If nothing else, anyone still half asleep would be sure to wake up. I am here to reconcile childhood with the land, and load the weight of the land onto the shoulders of the one who works it.

Somebody called to me. "Mahtab!" I walk toward the voice, a horde of children making a clamor around me: "No, the movies! No, no, the zoo!"

I opened the package. Inside there was a video cassette with a familiar photograph on the case. Hospital walls, drawn all over with little faded suns. *The Cold Sun.* A film by Mikhail Malnikov, director of *White Gold*, based on the life of Mahtab...

I clap my hands to get the children's attention. "Well? Have you decided? Where are we going? The movies, the Ferris wheel, or the zoo?"

"The zoo!"

"The movies!"

"No, that won't work. We'll have to vote. Who wants to go to the movies? Raise your hands!" I count. "Fourteen. All right, now who wants to go to the zoo? Let's see... Fifteen."

"Ohhhh! But that's only one vote more!" complains a movie lover.

"One person can have a very big influence on everything! Remember that. You've all just seen how one person was able to send us all to the zoo." They all laugh.

So do I. This is the first time I've woken up laughing. I don't know when I drifted off. Am I in Warsaw or Moscow? I look around me. There is a green telephone on the bedside table. I remembered asking them to give Nina-hanum a false message. I had lied. What about Lukasz? Had I dreamed him, or was he real? On the pillow to my left, there was a smudge of blood from his fingers.

I felt weightless, as if I had flapped my wings and was hovering right over the bed. I felt new, as if neither my heart nor my feet were tied to anything. There were no feelings inside me. No guilt, no offense, no complaints against anyone at all. I was free of the fetters of all my old worries. It was like walking out of the movie theater when a dark, difficult film is over. I was free, and I felt nothing. That is, until I picked up the phone and called Natasha.

After sobbing for a while, she said, "Don't hang up, please. Listen to me. I'm not crying because of you. I'm not worried about you at all. At least you can live with everything you remember or don't remember. But... But Mikhail has less than two months to live. Leukemia."

Natasha was the one who opened the door. She was holding a child, and there were tears of pain in her eyes. While she was telling me everything she had said over the phone again, her voice quiet and cracking, I looked into her little boy's light-blue eyes. Natasha wanted to be sure I hadn't forgotten—that Mikhail didn't want to see me. Natasha's embrace smelled like milk. Like the innocence of a child. "If he finds out you came, he'll be terribly angry at me. I promised him, you understand? Go quietly, and just for a second. He's not in good shape." She started to cry again. I walked into the bedroom.

The window was wide open. A thin, pale man was lying in the bed. A half-open mouth. Thin, dry lips. An old man, covered in wrinkles. If I hadn't seen the tattoo on his forearm, I never would have believed it was him.

Mama! Mikhail has dried up, too. Like the land and the sea. And there is no life left in the light-blue sun of his hands.

May 11, 2010.

About the Author

Shahzoda Samarqandi was born in Samarqand, Uzbekistan. Her taboo-breaking novels have brought her international recognition. After working for Tajik-language newspapers and television as well as the BBC Persian service, Samarqandi moved to the Netherlands where she served as an editor for Central Asia and Afghanistan at Radio Zamaneh, and she has worked to protect female activists and journalists in Afghanistan.

About the Translators

Shelley Fairweather-Vega is a full-time literary translator in Seattle, Washington, focusing on prose and poetry by today's best Central Asian writers. Mothersland was originally written in Tajik, a Persian language. This English translation was created from Persian translator Yultan Sadykova's lyrical Russian version. Sadykova holds a degree from Moscow State University and has translated contemporary Persian-language poetry and novels into Russian as well as Russian poetry from the Silver Age and 20th century into Persian. She lives in Tehran.